POUR BOY

P.J. DEVERE

Copyright © 2019 P.J. DeVere

Published by: Wicked & Cute Publishing, LLC

No part of this book may be reproduced, scanned, copied, or distributed in any printed or electronic form without written permission from the author. Please respect the author's rights and purchase only authenticated editions.

This is a work of fiction. Names, characters, places, and incidents are either the product of the author's imagination or are used fictitiously, and any resemblance to actual persons, living or dead, business establishments, events, or locales is entirely coincidental. The publisher does not have any control over and does not assume any responsibility for third-party websites or their content.

All rights reserved.

ISBN-13: 978-1-964218-02-1

For my husband, who doesn't complain about all the sexy men I write

1

"Ouch!" I scream at my boyfriend after he hits me square in the face with one of my thongs he has slingshot across my bedroom. I narrow my eyes at him, trying to express the severity of the trouble he is in with me. It doesn't work.

"Sorry," Patrick says, laughing and not looking at all sorry. "I didn't realize they had so much spring to them." He walks over and kisses the tip of my nose to make amends before sweeping the offending garment off the floor and into my suitcase.

"I wouldn't mind if that were the only thing you packed for our entire week away. They don't call it the Big Easy for nothing." He pulls me into his arms, and I can't be mad at him anymore. He's too damn cute.

"Oh, you expect me to be easy in New Orleans?" I thread my arms over his broad shoulders and pull him closer to me.

"Dawson, sweetheart. You are smart, you are beautiful, and you are the sexiest woman I've ever met... but trust me when I say you have never been easy."

He laughs at his own joke. Pretending to laugh with him, I step on his toe before rising to kiss his lips. Grunting in pain, he lifts me off my feet.

"You're such a bad girl."

"I do try."

Patrick brings his mouth down to mine again, walking us backward the few steps to my bed.

I break our kiss only long enough to reach behind him and knock my suitcase onto the floor, making room for us. Sitting on the edge of my bed, he pulls me on top of him--so much for getting packed up before dinner tonight.

His strong hands slide down the sides of my slinky dress. Although I was ready to walk out the door for our date, something tells me we'll be leaving later than I thought.

Patrick reaches the hem, and the dress moves with his hands back up my body, exposing me to his gaze. He pauses long enough to bring his eyes up to mine as if daring me to stop him, but I have no intention of putting the brakes on what is about to happen. I love this man, and I can't get enough of him.

After my dress is discarded somewhere over my shoulder, I work on unbuttoning his shirt while he's reclining back on his arms, watching me.

"I thought you wanted me ready for our date tonight and my suitcase packed for us to leave early tomorrow," I say innocently. He should know by now I'm not going to be the one to stop. If he wants us to leave on time, he will have to be the voice of reason because I am already lost to the idea of having him.

His eyes continue to scan me as he slowly shakes his head back and forth. "I will never tell you to take your hands off me, sweetheart."

The devilish grin he's wearing lets me know he thinks he

won. He's getting to have his way with me even though I was in the middle of packing for our trip. He doesn't realize that he has never looked sexier than he does right now, and I want him more than I want air.

I stop to unhook my strapless bra before going back to work on his shirt. Heat flashes in his eyes as he takes in the sight of my exposed breasts, and I delight in the fact that although he has seen them before and from every possible angle, they still have this effect on him.

Either I must not have been making good enough time in his clothes-removal department, or seeing me almost naked has spawned a new sense of urgency because his hands take over. With me still straddling his lap, Patrick engages his abs into a continuous sit-up position and makes quick work of the remaining buttons.

Goddamn it, that is hot. With a light touch, I rake my nails down his straining abdominal muscles and watch them jump, loving the feel of him underneath me. There's something about watching them move and flex that flat-out does it for me. There's no other way to say it—this man is beautiful.

Even with his shirt in a heap on top of my purple dress, Patrick is still more dressed than I am, seeing as I only have on my panties while he still has on his pants. Well, I did have on my panties. Without warning, he scoops me up, and when I land back on the bed, the only thing I have on are my diamond earrings. Soon after, his pants join the clothes heap.

I'm lying on the bed, watching him as he strokes himself. My knees part in an invitation, and his gaze travels down my body to land between them. Stalking me like a predator, he gets onto the bed and crawls up my body. When he makes it to my face, I fist my hand in his light brown hair as he hovers over me.

"You are so fucking sexy," he says into my ear in his low, rumbling voice.

Me? No, I'm awkward and nerdy and a perpetual klutz. Hell, I almost killed myself not too long ago when I brought him a basket of muffins and tripped into his kitchen with enough forward momentum to have broken my face had he not caught me in time.

As if he can read my thoughts, he raises my chin to make me look at him. "You, Dawson Everly, are the sexiest woman I have ever known. Never doubt that."

"Swoon."

He raises an eyebrow and laughs at me. "You're supposed to do it, not say it."

"I'll work on that." I put my hand on the back of his head and bring it down for another scorching hot kiss.

We're several months into our relationship, and everything is so perfect it scares me. Every second I don't have this man, I crave him.

I live in the small cottage in Patrick's backyard, so I've been spoiled with easy access to him. If I had it my way, we'd spend all this next week locked in a hotel room, leaving the "Do Not Disturb" sign hanging from the knob and getting noise complaints from the neighbors.

Tonight is the first night of Patrick's vacation time, but we won't leave for New Orleans until tomorrow morning. However, he is taking me out to dinner at some fancy restaurant in town this evening before we start our road trip tomorrow morning, so technically, our vacation has begun.

Pour Boy

Patrick made a late dinner reservation for us. I think we both knew he couldn't resist swinging by his bar to check on everything one more time before we leave town—he's the worst helicopter parent when it comes to Study. I'm a little overdressed to hang out at his bar, but I don't mind. I've found that after a few screaming orgasms, there isn't much I do mind.

I find my usual bar stool and order my vodka gimlet while Patrick heads to the back to be sure everything is running as it should be. Patrick's twin brother, Jameson, is the bartender tonight, so I talk with him while I wait for my two best friends, Alex and Bridget, who said they were going to pop by.

Patrick and I have Jameson to thank for being able to get out of town for a little while. He stepped up, offered to help, and practically forced Patrick to take this time off with me. He knew we needed a break, but that means Jameson will be working his ass off. This week will be nonstop for him since he'll be trying cases in court all day and bartending all night, but he wanted to do this for his brother. For years, they weren't close at all, but their relationship has turned a corner and has become something I think they both needed.

"My, my, aren't we all dressed up? Is the band that good?" Alex says as she and Bridget grab some barstools next to me. I'm happy to see them, but I also feel guilty for not spending as much time with them as I should have over the last few months.

Between having the summer off from teaching at the college and my whirlwind romance with Patrick, I may have been that girl who neglects her friends in favor of her hot new boyfriend.

With that being acknowledged, I will need at least one

more week of their compassion and understanding because the only thing I'm doing from now until I get back from New Orleans is Mr. Patrick Butler. Remembering our vigorous romp in the bedroom, I reach up to be sure my diamond earrings are still secure. I look down at the dress I had to steam the wrinkles out of before putting it back on, and I smile to myself.

"As much as I love The Velvet Ditches, no. They did not inspire this dress. My handsome boyfriend is treating me to some much-needed fun and adventure."

"But tonight, you're with us?" Bridget asks.

"Not for long. We have reservations for dinner, and we leave tomorrow to spend a few days in New Orleans. My summer session ended, so I'm free until August. Between Jameson and me, we were able to twist Patrick's arm and make him take some time off, so we've got a little road trip planned."

Bridget pouts, but Alex puts her hand on my arm and leans in to be heard over the music. "When you get back, you belong to us for at least two nights of girl time." She's not asking, and there's no room for argument.

"Yes, ma'am. You've got me as soon as I return. I promise." That seems to satisfy them.

I look around and realize I haven't seen Jameson behind the bar since the girls came in and sat down beside me. I guess he's in the back helping Patrick. Alex orders a round of drinks from Nate, the other bartender, and we fall into easy conversation.

"Who is going to help Nate handle this kind of crowd? Doesn't Patrick help him tend the bar on nights like these?" Alex asks, swirling the glass of wine in her hand.

"He's got some help. Exel said he could work a few night shifts, but it will mainly be Jameson."

Alex takes another sip. "Interesting."

I figure the real reason for her question was to determine how often Jameson will be bartending this week. They have some kind of past together, but she doesn't talk about it.

"Will Exel be 'busy' with Madeline?"

I assume Alex's question is her attempt to move the subject off Jameson before we pry deeper, but that's fine. This isn't the first time I've had to field a question about Madeline's love life.

It hasn't taken my sister long to become a legend in this small town. An introvert she is not, and I wouldn't be the least bit surprised to find people had betting pools going as to when she and Exel will get together.

"I don't think she's climbed that particular mountain yet. If she has, she hasn't told me about it. No, I think Exel had something else to do tonight." As I answer her, I realize I haven't had a lot of conversations with Mads in the last few weeks, either. We see each other, but I've got to schedule some quality bonding time soon.

"Whatever will your sister do without you around?" Bridget asks me.

"If I'm honest, my sister hasn't been around all that much. Mads said she is keeping her distance until the sickeningly sweet new-lust stage wears off between Patrick and me. If that's really the case, I may never see her again because I can't imagine it changing."

Some nights, Madeline still stays at my cottage behind Patrick's house when I stay over at his place, some nights she sleeps over at Henry's, and some nights she's unaccounted for. Those are the nights we need to spend some sister time talking about. That girl was born with a head full of wild hair.

Alex has no idea that what she's heard is just the tip of the iceberg if I know Madeline... and I know Madeline. "Mads keeps herself more than occupied whether I'm around or not. A little too occupied since her breakup if you ask me."

Alex is quick to come to her defense. "Maybe she's trying to find herself?"

I pick up my vodka gimlet and take another sip. I'm not a prude, but even I have raised an eyebrow over some rumors about her latest romantic adventures.

"Then she might be going about it the wrong way unless she's misplaced herself down a random guy's pants."

"Well, it is always in the last place you look," Bridget says with a straight face, making me giggle.

"Can I get you lovely ladies anything else?" Jameson is back and standing on the other side of the bar, looking directly at Alex.

She seems surprised to see him, and I guess that's my fault for not mentioning he's working tonight. I imagine most people here assume it's Patrick pouring their drinks and not his identical twin. Alex is one of the few people besides me who can tell one brother apart from the other at first glance.

"J, when did you become a bartender?" Alex asks him.

"That's Jameson? How the hell can you tell those two apart?" Bridget asks.

"Oh, that's easy," Jameson answers before Alex or I get the chance. "I'm the cute one. The less attractive brother needed some help tonight, and I needed to get out of the house."

I take another sip of my gimlet and zone out of their conversation as my mind wanders back to an hour or so ago. I'm glad no one can see the X-rated scene I'm reliving in my mind right now. It's a play-by-play from earlier, and it's getting me all hot and bothered. My dress feels heavy as I imagine Patrick's hands running the length of it again. I have to re-cross my legs to alleviate some of the ache slowly building inside me.

Through my lust-hazed vision, I watch Patrick as he comes out of the back room. When our eyes meet, he recognizes the look on my face. I lick my lips, and it causes his pace to falter a step before he makes it to my side of the bar. His little stumble gives me a warped sense of pride that I can make him react like this, and I don't hide the smile it puts on my face.

Patrick winks at me before looking around at our group as he approaches, and his eyes settle on Jameson. They must be doing a twin telepathic communication thing because they both look like they're trying to send the other some kind of message.

"It's crazy who all you can catch up with in one night of bartending. Isn't it, brother?" Patrick finally says as he slides between my two friends to stand beside me. Jameson raises his middle finger, flipping Patrick off before walking down to the other end of the bar to take orders from the new customers.

"Well, that was rude," Bridget points out.

"He's had a rough couple of weeks," Patrick explains as he flags down Nate to get a drink since his brother is now ignoring him.

As we visit with my friends, Patrick slips his arm around my shoulders and pulls me close to him. I'm trying to concentrate on what everyone is saying, but I can't seem to make myself listen. Leaning back into Patrick, my mind is fuzzy with desire as I smell the cologne on his neck and feel him so close to me.

I want to ask him what he knows about Jameson and Alex, but I forget everything in my head when he leans over and whispers in my ear, "Fuck the reservation. Let's go back to my place."

Looks like we have some telepathic communication, also.

2

"Is that everything? You know we're only going for a week, right?" Patrick asks as he watches me roll my second suitcase to his SUV.

"Alright, I may have gone overboard. I've never been to New Orleans, so I had no idea what to pack."

Patrick takes the case from me and slides it into his vehicle. "It's summer, and it's a thousand degrees. You can get by wearing little to nothing." He grabs me and pulls me in for a kiss as hot as the weather. "If we're lucky, maybe we'll catch a naked bike ride parade."

I laugh, but he doesn't. "Wait. Are you kidding?"

"I can't believe you've never been to New Orleans." This is the third time he's mentioned that this morning.

"I told you. I grew up close to Memphis, and we had Beale Street. I never saw the point."

He shakes his head before kissing me again. I return his kiss, but I can't help but think in the back of my mind, *naked bike rides? Where the hell is he taking me?*

I run back into his kitchen and grab two disposable coffee cups. Setting them down on the counter, I empty what's left of the brewed coffee equally between them. I add some cream to my coffee, but I know he likes his black. I should have given his cup more because mine is as full as it can be after adding cream.

Since my cup is almost overflowing, I don't secure the lid. I slap the top on his and hold the top to mine between my teeth as I maneuver both cups out the door.

"You're my hero," he says, taking a long swig. Neither of us got much sleep last night, but it was well worth the REM sacrifice. Here's hoping this caffeine makes up for it.

Patrick must be thinking along the same lines I am when he says, "It's going to be a long drive on no sleep, but I wouldn't take back a second of the hours we stayed up last night."

I hold my coffee out to the side as steady as I can, stand on my tiptoes, and give him another kiss reminiscent of the night we just spent together.

"Jesus, you make it hard to leave the house," he growls into my ear.

"That's okay. I can make it just as hard for you in the car, if you know what I mean." I wink at him before opening the passenger's side door.

He walks around to the driver's side and adjusts himself before getting in and starting our long journey south.

I grab his hand off the steering wheel and bring it over for a quick kiss on his knuckles. I do love this man. I haven't told him yet, but I feel it every second I'm with him. I let out a happy sigh as we leave the driveway. This is going to be a great trip.

I pull down the visor and flip up the cover on the tiny mirror. What I see in the reflection has me grabbing my makeup bag out of my purse. I need to reapply the lipstick

Pour Boy

Patrick kissed off my face this morning, and that's what I'm doing when he scares the ever-loving shit out of me.

"Oh, my God! Your coffee is everywhere!" His voice booms through the car.

I put my hand over my heart to settle the poor sucker down and scan the area for danger before his words make it through my brain, and I realize there is no emergency. I glance back to the mirror at the line of lipstick he caused me to draw up the side of my cheek and swat his arm.

"Patrick! You gave me a heart attack!"

I open his glove compartment and grab some of his neatly stacked napkins. I've just started to remove the red streak from my cheek when he takes them out of my hand to clean up the few drops of coffee that have spilled around my cup.

"Are you serious right now?" I ask him, holding my hand up, which no longer holds a napkin.

"Are you serious right now?" he answers, still blotting where the spill had been. I open the console to grab another napkin and continue cleaning up my face while trying to control my temper.

I've ridden with him in the past, but those drives were always quick trips around town. Thinking back, I don't recall ever bringing anything to eat or drink into his vehicle before today. Yes, I know he keeps his vehicle spotless. Yes, I know he is obsessive about it. Yes, this is probably the first thing ever to be spilled in it, but it is not that big of a deal. It's a few drops at the most.

He seems angrier than I believe this situation calls for. He's at an eleven when he should be at a zero-point five at best. I would never shout or give my passengers the silent treatment if they spilled something in my car.

His hands are gripping the wheel, and his jaw is tight. I

don't get what the big deal is, but on the other hand, I don't treat my vehicle like the inside of an operating room. He puts the top on my coffee, and we drive for a while without speaking before I break.

If it takes a little apologizing to have a good first road trip together, so be it. I swallow my pride and do what needs to be done. "Babe, I'm sorry I spilled the coffee. I should have held it until I could have put the top on it."

I watch his shoulders relax and hope I'm in the clear. I wait for the "No worries" or, for the even better, "I'm sorry, too. I overreacted."

Instead, I get a gentle, "You have to be more careful if you want to eat and drink in Bev."

My eyebrows shoot up my face. Did this man just speak to me like I'm a child instead of the glorious grown-ass woman I am? I'm not sure what to cover first.

"Excuse me? What do you mean 'if I want to eat and drink?' ...and did you say Bev? What the hell is a Bev?"

"Bev, as in Beverly. She's who you're riding in right now, and she doesn't like to be sticky." He pats the dashboard like he's petting the cat.

"She's the only one I'm going to be riding," I mutter under my breath. I'm not sure if he's kidding with me or if he's serious. Either way, it is too early in the morning for this. I look out the window, wondering if I stepped into an alternate reality.

I'm trying to wrap my mind around how our first fight ever in all the months we've been together is over spilled coffee, how he could be so condescending, and how I ended up with this obsessive maniac when he looks over at me and dares to smile.

He must have taken my silence and puzzled expression

as a sign that I'm fine with the sudden rise of the patriarchy in the confines of Bev because he reaches over to turn on the radio as if all is right in the world.

I didn't think this ride could get worse, but boy, was I wrong.

Banjos.

Fiddles.

So many banjos and fiddles.

I look to see what radio station is playing this mean-spirited prank on its listeners, and I realize it's connected to his phone. He is choosing for us to hear what we're hearing right now. This audial assault is on purpose.

"Patrick, sweetheart. What are we listening to?" I want to plug my ears, but I settle for turning the volume down a few notches.

"It's a new bluegrass group called the Foggy Holler Mountain Cats. I'm thinking of booking them for Study."

He reaches over to turn the music back up, but I place my hand on his, stopping him.

"Because you're trying to go out of business? Babe, there are easier ways to shut the place down." I turn the volume down more.

"No way, Dawson. These guys are great! You haven't heard enough to judge them. Why don't you tell me what you think of them at the end of the album?"

At the end of the... what? Nope. There is no chance I'm going to make it to the end of this album without hurling myself onto the freeway in the hopes some merciful eighteen-wheeler's grille will snuff me out of my misery.

He turns the music back up, and I can swear my ear holes are trying to close themselves off in self-defense.

"These mountain cats, are they rabid, or is there a leg

caught in a trap?" My question comes out distorted as I've put my hands over my face to muffle the impending scream. I've just diagnosed myself with misophonia.

I'm guessing the "fog" part of Foggy Mountain is the thick marijuana haze someone would have to hot box incubate themselves in before they could stand to listen to this quasi-abusive whining set to banjos, fiddles, and what I can only imagine is foot-stomping. Patrick doesn't seem to be having the same difficulties as me. I watch as his hand bumps his leg to its unrelenting rhythm.

Four songs in, and not only am I questioning whether or not I know my boyfriend, but I am done. I am done listening to this noise, and I don't care if he's enjoying himself and wants me to experience something with him that makes him happy. I'm not that good of a person.

"Okay! My turn to pick the music!" I scream out. I try to sound upbeat and happy, but I'm afraid it comes off more as maniacal and crazy.

He stops me before I can reach it. "Sorry, babe. The person driving is the person in charge of the radio." He shrugs as if he has no control over it.

"Then pull over 'babe' because I'm driving." I unbuckle my seatbelt before he can stop me.

"Oh, no. No, no, no. I'm the only one who drives Bev."

I need help picking my jaw off the floor. He has got to be joking. "You know, you let me drive her before, right?" I cross my arms over my chest in smug satisfaction, knowing I made a solid point and there is no way he can argue. The night I saw my now ex-husband in Starkford, Patrick tossed me his keys, and I drove to his dad's house in the pouring rain.

"Yeah, I remember, and I also remember it taking a week

to get all the mud stains out. Besides, that was an emergency, so it doesn't count. I'm the only one Bev trusts." He rubs a loving hand over the dash again, and I roll my eyes.

"Uh-huh. You're telling me whoever drives gets to pick the music, and you're the only one who can drive. That's not going to work for me, cowboy." My seatbelt alarm is dinging like crazy, adding a whole new level of get-me-the-fuck-out-of-this-car to the situation.

"Dawson, I'm not trying to be difficult, but I feel like you haven't given them a chance. Plus, I have to listen to the whole album to know whether or not to book them. It's for work."

He seems calm and patient, but I'm ready to pull my hair out. "Every song so far has sounded the same! How are you not getting the gist?—Here, I'll sum up the whole album for you!" I say louder than intended as I lean closer to him. I mimic what I think banjo playing looks like and stamp my feet like a crazy person as I shout, "Plink, Plink, YEE-HAW, Stomp, Stomp!" followed by blowing two raspberries in his face.

I stop my rant without him saying a word, but I don't move back into my seat. I'm two inches from his face with my air banjo in hand.

I hold the stare he gives me, even though his eyes go back and forth between looking at the road and me. I'm hyper-aware of the spittle strand that has settled on my left upper lip, but it'll have to wait. I'm not losing this staring contest.

After a moment, Patrick bursts out laughing, and I follow soon after. He reaches over and turns the volume all the way down as he shakes his head at my silly antics. "Put on whatever music you want, sweetheart. It's all yours."

I smile as I connect my phone to his radio. Did I overreact at having to listen to his music? Probably, but the important thing to remember is it was successful. I'll file that episode of crazy under "Whatever Works" and enjoy the better music we're about to have.

3

We pull up to the French Royal Inn in the early afternoon, but I want Patrick to drive us around New Orleans for a few more hours because I've never seen anything like it. I roll my windows down and take in everything I can, from shotgun houses and townhouses with wrought iron balconies to sprawling mansions with live oak trees—this place is amazing.

When we get into the French Quarter, I hear a brass band playing Louis Armstrong's "A Kiss to Build a Dream On," and I look over at Patrick with the biggest grin on my face. "I can't wait to explore this whole city."

"It's different and the same every time I come here. You're going to love it."

We get out at our hotel, and the valet takes Bev. I shoot Patrick a look to let him know I saw him hand over his precious baby's keys to another person, but he ignores me.

When we go to the lobby to check in, we get detailed instructions on how to get to our room, which I think is strange until I walk out the back door and into a breathtaking courtyard surrounded by individual buildings. With these beautiful balconies and so much French charm, I've stepped back in time. There is a postage stamp-sized pool in the middle of the stone floor that looks good enough to jump into right now, especially since the temperature is somewhere around a hundred degrees.

Patrick points to a building on our right, and we go inside and find our room. It's spacious with high ceilings, huge windows, and heavy, opulent curtains. It's also filled with antique furniture, from the four-post king-sized bed to the vintage lamps on the nightstands.

"I feel like I'm in a movie."

"Yeah, this place is one of my favorites."

I walk into the ensuite bathroom and find a clawfoot tub next to a large vanity. I grab my makeup bag from my purse and am freshening up in the mirror when Patrick puts his arms around me from behind and kisses my neck.

"Ready to have your first beignet?"

I turn and smile up at him. "Is that a code word for something else?" I wrap my arms around his neck and run my fingers through his hair. I don't care we weren't the best version of ourselves on our ride down here. We're here now, together, and that's what matters. This man is what matters.

"Now it is," he says with a mischievous gleam in his eye.

"Then I need you to beignet the hell out of me, Mr. Butler."

I jump into his arms and wrap my legs around his waist, makeup forgotten. He puts his hands on my ass to support me while he gives me a kiss that leaves no doubt in my mind about where this is heading.

He turns and places me on the vanity with him standing between my legs, and I'm happy to discover it's the perfect height for what we're about to do.

He fishes a condom out of his wallet, and he undoes his

jeans. God, why do I get so turned on watching him do that? I pull the elastic on his boxer briefs and slip my hand into them to find he's already hard for me. When I stroke him, his head rolls back, and he moans a low, guttural sound that instantly has me wet for him.

I don't want him to know how needy I am, even if I'm not doing the best job at disguising it. "We can stop. Anytime you want to stop, just say when."

I don't mean what I say and don't have any intention of stopping. I only say that to make him think I'm more in control than I am. Truth be told, I have completely fallen for this man, and the last thing I want to happen is for him to stop touching me.

His eyes are half-closed with desire as I continue to stroke him. "Sweetheart, if we never leave this room the entire time we're here, that would be more than fine by me. You're all I need. I mean that Dawson, you here with me—whether we're talking, making love, fighting, or fucking—you are all I need in this world to be happy."

I take my hands away long enough to prop myself on the counter. I make a pointed look at my shorts and raise one eyebrow at him, and it doesn't take him long to understand what I want him to do. He takes hold of the top of my shorts, and I lift my hips, allowing him to bring them and my panties down and off me.

"Fast and hard or slow and sweet?" He cups his hand over my mound before and rubs before sliding two fingers in and out of me. I know he can tell how ready I am for him. I want him every way I can get him, but he wants me to decide the pace for us. While I would love nothing more than to spend the rest of the night wrapped around him, I do want to see at least some of the city while I'm here.

"Fast and hard."

"You got it," he says into my ear in a low whisper, gripping me under my thighs and pulling me closer to him. His hand reaches between us to guide him inside me, and we both moan with pleasure when he enters.

After a few thrusts, he wraps his arms around my waist and picks me up while he's still buried deep inside. He moves my body up and down his cock several times before he turns and props my back against the wall, and it's the sexiest thing I've ever experienced in my life.

There's no controlling the noises I'm making, and I don't care who hears me. My legs are wrapped tightly around his waist, and his hands are holding my hips as he moves me in time with his driving rhythm.

I bring my hand to the back of his neck and pull him in for a kiss—It's reckless. Hot blooded. Patrick is on fire for me, and that turns me on even more. His mouth plunders mine before sliding down my neck, licking and sucking his way to my shoulder. He is feral right now, taking pleasure from me as I'm getting it from him. We're both running on our primal, basic instincts as we writhe and move together. This is how I love Patrick the most, completely lost to everything in the world except me.

I'm so close, but I don't want this to end. I feel my orgasm building inside me, and I clench around him. He lightly bites my shoulder as he lets out a groan. The sounds he's making put me over the edge.

Patrick raises his head and puts his lips where they're almost touching mine. His green eyes are drunk with lust as he continues to move inside of me.

"Come for me, sweetheart. I want to hear you."

One more thrust from Patrick and I shatter. My arms and legs grip him harder, and I hold on as I ride him through some of the most intense pleasure I've ever experienced.

After I come down from that high, I try to catch my breath. He's still buried to the hilt inside of me as I shake around him.

"Better?"

My head rests on his chest, and I'm not sure I remember how to use words. I manage to say, "Much."

He starts to move us away from the wall, and I cling to him tighter. "You can't put me down yet. My legs won't work."

He walks us out of the bathroom and toward the bed. "Sweetheart, I won't be putting you down for a while. We're not even close to done."

"Swoon."

And I do mean 'swoon.' My head falls back, and I use my leg muscles to move myself up and down his shaft. He's like a drug. Even after that soul melting climax, I want him again.

He rumbles out a deep laugh as he lays us down on the bed. "You're getting better at that. This time, you said it, and you did it."

It's a couple of hours before we make it out the door and walk to Café Du Monde. There is a line down the sidewalk to get in, and I pull Patrick's hand in the other direction, signaling I'd like to abort this mission. I want to experience New Orleans and don't want to wait an hour or two in line for a pastry.

Patrick looks at the line of people and shakes his head. "Tourists."

I stop trying to pull him away. "What do you mean 'tourists?' We're tourists, too."

He leads me around to the back of the seating area. "No, I've been here enough to know what's up. Do you see that group blocking the main entrance? Those people are politely waiting for someone to seat them. That's not how this place works."

We go in from the back and find several empty tables. "It's first come, first served here," he says as he smiles at our waitress. He asks her for two orders of beignets and two café au laits.

I'm surprised when it arrives to see he ordered himself a coffee with cream. "I thought you liked your coffee without anything in it?"

He takes a small sip and closes his eyes in delight. "You haven't had anything like this before. There's chicory mixed in with the coffee. Mmm, so good," he says, taking another sip.

It looks piping hot, so I'll try my beignets first. I balance the mound of powdered sugar as I lift it for a bite, but as soon as my teeth sink in, the powdered sugar goes straight up my nose and down my windpipe.

I cough furiously, covering both of us with a fine white mist and attracting the attention of our neighboring tables. Embarrassed, I look at Patrick.

He's laughing at me. "I forgot to warn you. Don't breathe while you're eating these."

I'm so glad he's having such a good time. After I've evacuated the majority of the powdery substance from my nasal passages and throat, I look down at the cute black tank top I'm wearing and see it's destroyed.

"We've got to go back to the room."

His eyes look me up and down as he licks a bit of

powdered sugar from his top lip. "You want me again so soon? I'm not a man who will tell you no, but you'll never get to see New Orleans at this rate."

I make a face to let him know that is not what I meant.

"You'll be fine, princess. You don't need to change clothes over that."

I pick up a large pinch of sugar between my fingers and throw it on his t-shirt. Now I'm the one laughing, "Oops, looks like you'll need to change, too, 'princess.'"

He looks down at his shirt, now doused with sugar. Without a word, he picks up the teaspoon that was delivered with our coffees, scoops up some sugar, and puts it in the palm of his hand.

"Don't you dare!" I yell as he holds it up to his mouth and blows it in my direction. We're both laughing as I try to swat the airborne particles down.

He grabs a napkin and hands it to me. "This is all we need." He takes another napkin, dips the end in the small cup of water sitting on the table, and helps me clean up. Once there's more sugar on the table than on me, we get up and hit the French Market.

"Let's stay in," I beg him once we get back to the room that evening. The unrelenting heat has beaten me down, and my feet are tired from exploring the city all day. We rode streetcars, ate crawfish étouffée, went to a museum... We came, we saw, we conquered.

"Are you kidding? The whole point of New Orleans is the nightlife. You haven't lived until you've seen the French Quarter at night. Besides, after we do the Quarter, I plan to take you to some local places I've discovered throughout the years on the rest of our nights here."

"What if we started tomorrow and stayed in tonight? We've got all week. We can ease our way into it."

"Sweetheart, we now have less than a week, so we're going to check off the obligatory Bourbon Street tonight. Trust me. I've got so many other places I'm dying to take you, so we don't need to miss out by staying in."

Sprawled out on top of the bed, I open one eye and look at him. "How many times have you been down here?"

Patrick laughs, "You mean the ones I have clear memories of? Hmm… even those are quite a few. Don't worry. You have an excellent tour guide. No one knows this city better than me."

We are almost crawling back to our room in the early morning hours.

"Why didn't you tell me how powerful hurricanes are?" I am going to have one mother of a headache tomorrow.

"I don't want to hear about your silly-ass hurricanes. How could you let me do shots?"

We are supporting each other upright as I fumble through my purse for the door key. Once I clumsily open the door, we both make it to the bed and lie on our backs.

"Why did you make me sing karaoke?" he asks through his slurred speech.

"Make you?" I turn to look at him. "I couldn't stop you. I'll never hear Taylor Swift the same way again."

I smile, thinking about Patrick on stage—belting out songs at the top of his lungs. What he lacked in skill, he made up for in confidence, and he had never been sexier.

I stifle a giggle when I picture one particular high note when he raised himself on his toes and threw his hands out to help himself hit it. Patrick must have guessed what has me giggling. His hand comes over and tries to tickle my side, but I playfully swat him away.

He quits his attempts to get at me, and we are quiet for a moment. Being this still only serves to amplify how drunk I feel. It's like my head is bobbing in imaginary water.

"Make it stop," I tell him.

"Make what stop?"

"The room." I cover my eyes with my hand, but it doesn't help.

"Well, you know what they say. If you can't make the Earth move, make the room spin."

I laugh, and it sends me into another dimension. I hold onto the bed for support.

"I'd say, 'why not make the Earth move while the room spins,' but I'm afraid I'd vomit on you," I whisper to him through my dizziness.

He doesn't respond, and his rhythmic breathing leads me to believe he has fallen asleep. My eyes also shut, and I'm about to ride this inebriated wave into dreamland when...

"I'd still love you."

My eyes pop open. He'd still what?

Holy Mother of God, did he just say he loves me? For the first time ever? While we are drunk off our asses and smelling like Bourbon Street?

Did he say it on purpose?

I try to sit up, but that is a spectacularly bad idea. My brain has had too much alcohol to process what had to have been a drunken slip-up on his part.

Our deal from the beginning was to take this slow, and "I

love you" always means more than "I love you." It means commitment. Commitment leads to more serious things like moving in together. Moving in together leads to marriage, and marriage could lead to trying to have children.

I tried with my first husband, but it never happened. I now understand that was a blessing, but it was still a very hard time in my life. I don't know if I'm ready to ride down that road again so soon. The first time, that road's potholes turned out to be landmines. At the end of it, I was pulled from a fiery crash that almost took my sanity.

I look over to see Patrick, who has fallen asleep facing me. Instead of freaking out, I should remember how much he helped me through that terrible time. He looks so peaceful when he's sleeping. I could say those words back to him right now, and he wouldn't hear me. I'd be the only one who knew I'd said it, but I'm not ready for the change that would bring, even if the only thing it would change is me. I can feel the feeling, but I won't be the first to say it on purpose.

I make an effort to stay conscious, but it's no use. I'm a goner. As I fall asleep, a small, helpless part of me realizes we are both still on top of the covers, fully clothed, and with a layer or two of Bourbon Street grime coating us. I feel gross, but it is not enough to do anything about it when my body finds this comfy spot on the bed.

We'll ask the hotel to burn the comforter tomorrow.

4

We sleep well into the afternoon and take our time showering, hydrating, and getting ready for the evening. I choose my favorite blue strapless dress with nude sandals, and I pin my hair on top of my head, letting a few strands hang down to frame my face. It looks great, and Patrick seems to like it, but the real reason for all these choices is to help keep me cool in this sweltering city. The dead heat of summer might not have been the best time to visit.

We ride the streetcar to the Garden District, and I am in love with the beautiful houses and neighborhoods. There's still some light left in the day, so I soak in everything I see as we travel through each charming street. We get off at our stop and walk a few blocks to the restaurant Patrick has been excited about going to all day.

Thinking we have arrived, I reach for the door, but he stops me.

"Not here. This place is a bit more out of the way." He guides me around the corner and through a wrought iron gate.

We follow a flagstone pathway flanked on each side by a wild, thick mass of green plants, which seems magical in the twilight. Lanterns hang on four-foot-tall poles and are placed every few feet or so down the path, lighting our way. When we get to the door, there is a small sign hanging above it with the name "Envie."

"They spelled it wrong," I joke before we go inside.

"No, they didn't. It's a Cajun word. It means to have a hankering."

"A hankering?"

"Yeah, as in a deep desire for something—a craving." Without warning, he pulls my body into his. With his lips touching mine, he whispers, "Like the world will end if you don't have it."

I meet his intense, hungry stare for a moment before he kisses me. We make out like two teenagers in the middle of the pathway, and I'm unsteady on my feet when he pulls away.

I reach up to adjust my lipstick. "Hankering. Got it."

I clear my throat and adjust my clothing before we make our way inside. It smells like French bread and happiness when we open the door, and I realize I'm starving. We haven't had anything substantial to eat since last night. Patrick and I follow the hostess by the fairy lights hanging on the ceiling to find our table, and I take a moment to look around.

There are a handful of tables dotted between low-backed chairs and sofas. It's as if someone took a coffee shop, a bar, and a restaurant and smashed them all into one beautiful old building. Just as many people are here enjoying an evening cocktail or latté as there are those who came for dinner.

The place is narrow, and the focal point is the ornate

antique bar, which takes up the entirety of one long wall. Liquor bottles in every color imaginable look like they are lit from within as they sit on shelf after expertly-carved shelf. There's a mirror in the dead center of the bar that shows its age, while the wood around it gleams as if it's polished by hand every hour.

I laugh as I watch a little old lady shuffling around and guilting men into buying long-stemmed roses for their dates. Victim after victim take out their wallets, and the small woman smiles in triumph.

"That bar has got to be as old as New Orleans itself. I've never seen anything like this before," I say as I take in the whole scene.

"This is one of the oldest places in the city, and it has the best music, too." He points at a stage taking up one of the smaller walls. The piano, double bass, and drums are already manned, and they seem to be waiting for someone to occupy the space behind the vintage microphone.

We are not disappointed. A beautiful woman with dark skin and even darker hair takes the stage as if she owns it. Her dress is a deep red that sparkles under the lights, and she looks out at the audience like she has a secret. She starts to sing in a low, sultry tone, and the instruments tiptoe in behind her voice to join her. This is jazz at its best.

"Hi, I'm Candace. I'll be your server tonight." My attention is diverted to the woman standing at our table. If someone were to draw what sex looks like in female form, they'd draw her... or Jessica Rabbit.

Candace's voice has some exotic accent to it. That—along with her jet-black, wavy hair and red, glossy lips—makes her downright dangerous. The end of a rosary is tucked away inside her ample bosom, and I can only imagine she uses it to pray for the buttons on her white shirt that are having a difficult time containing her large breasts.

She sets her tray on the stand behind her before bending over our table to deliver a complimentary bowl of gumbo with a basket of bread medallions. Just when I think the cleavage show is over, she grabs some menus and shifts over to lean toward Patrick, giving him quite a view. Putting an arm on the back of his chair, she proceeds to talk to him like I'm not there. I can tell Patrick is making an effort not to stare at her chest, but she's not making this easy for any of us.

"It's great to have you here tonight. Take your time looking over all we have to offer," she coos at my boyfriend, putting both our menus in his hands.

"Thank you, Candace. We sure will," he says as he smiles up at her. At least he's still looking at her face.

She straightens and catches me eyeing how short her skirt is. Laughing, she says, "I know, we're supposed to wear tights, but it's too hot for anything underneath, don't you think?" She winks at Patrick before slinking away from our table.

As soon as she's out of earshot, Patrick starts to speak, but I beat him to it, "Okay, your new friend Candy needs to slide back up whatever stripper pole she came down because that was not cool, Patrick. Not cool at all."

He's laughing at me, but I give him a look to let him know I will shank a bitch. He takes my hand and kisses it. "You don't need to be jealous, sweetheart. You are the most beautiful woman in this room, and I only have eyes for you."

That was nice, but still. "I'm going to ask for another waitress, and I'm not jealous. She told us she's going commando. That has to be violating at least a dozen health code regulations."

He kisses my hand again. "There's no need to be jealous, and there's no need for another waitress. Please, trust me when I say you're the only woman I want."

"I do trust you, it's just—"

"It's just nothing. You trust me, or you don't, so—trust me." He knows the look he's giving me could charm the pants off a nun. I let out a long sigh.

"Fine. I trust you."

We manage to make it through our meal without any impromptu lap dances from our waitress, and I count that as a win. With our bellies full, we sit back and enjoy an after-dinner cocktail and the best jazz music I've ever heard. Between the smokiness in the singer's voice and the warmth from the bourbon in my old fashioned, I am as content as a cat with a soft place to curl up for a nap.

"Oh, no, thank you," I hear Patrick say to someone behind me. I turn around to see the little old lady carrying a basket of roses. Up close, she's even older than I thought.

When I first saw her, I let Patrick know he shouldn't give in if she asks him to buy me a flower because I don't want to carry it around the rest of the night. It seems I may have underestimated how intimidating she can be.

She looks Patrick up and down and makes a face like she's disgusted with him, which seems a bit harsh.

"This isn't about you, son," she rasps out before placing the entire basket of roses on the table in front of me. With a haughty harumph in his direction, she shuffles off toward the door to leave.

Patrick and I look at each other, each with one eyebrow raised in matching shock and confusion.

"I hope she's not going to go off herself. I would have bought a rose," he says, only halfway joking.

"Why would she leave all her roses and her basket on our table?" It's the obvious question we're both wondering.

"Because I bought them for you."

Patrick and I look up to see the man who has approached our table, and I can't believe my eyes.

"Shelly!" I scream in delight before jumping up and hugging him—hard. I'm still holding him tightly to me when I hear Patrick.

"And why did you buy my girlfriend," he stops to count, "over a dozen roses?"

My back stiffens, and I pull out of my embrace with my long-lost friend.

"Because that's all the lady had available for purchase?" Shelly answers as if he's asking a question in return.

I stifle a laugh, which doesn't help matters. Patrick doesn't seem to find him as funny as I do.

"And why did you buy my girlfriend roses at all?" he asks in a growl. He's livid and giving my friend the ultimate go-to-hell look. Do I love that he's jealous? If I'm honest, it turns me on, but I don't want him to be mean to my friend. The way Patrick is acting now, he might as well pee a circle around me to mark his territory, but it seems Shelly is taking his questions in stride.

"Why did I buy her roses? Because I didn't know what she was drinking."

Patrick's face shows he didn't like that answer any better than the last. I sit back down in my chair and send a subtle kick to my boyfriend's shin while smiling up at Shelly.

Pour Boy

"Please, sit. Join us. I haven't seen you in ages!" I extend the invitation without consulting Patrick.

Shelly looks at him and decides to ignore the disgruntled expression on his face. "Sure, I'd love to." He grabs a chair from another table and brings it to ours, taking a seat between Patrick and me.

"Oh gosh, Shel. It's been so long—I don't know where to start! It's been what—like, six years? I've kept up with you, though, and I'm so proud of you!"

Truth be told, I'm his biggest fan.

"How do you two know each other?" Patrick asks after figuring out this guy is here to stay for the time being.

"Dawson and I were classmates. We went through our Ph.D. program together." Shelly is answering Patrick, but his eyes never leave me.

"Oh, we were more than classmates. Shelly was my best friend. I would have never gotten through those years without him. Now he's a famous author! He writes those crazy thrillers I'm always reading. What are you doing here in New Orleans? Research for your next book?"

He looks at me like he used to with those big blue eyes. His chestnut brown hair is longer on top than how he wore it in school, but he still looks like my Shelly. The shiny locks used to fall down onto his forehead, but now he has them swept to the side. His dark-rimmed glasses are an upgrade from the nerdy ones he wore in college, and I have to admit, he looks great.

"I live here now. I moved about four years ago. I grew up here, so it was more about coming back home."

He stands up to signal the bartender to send him a drink with nothing more than a slight wave of his hand, so he seems to be a regular. As he stands, I notice a lot more lean muscle on him than he had back in our college days. I wonder how else he's changed through the years. I feel bad I didn't make more of an effort to stay in touch with him. Once he got so successful, it was difficult to reach out to him, but I should have tried harder.

It's no time at all before our waitress brings him a small amount of something amber in a crystal rocks glass. He hands her some cash and stops her when she starts to give him change. After she walks away, we start to talk about our years in college and where life has taken us when Patrick seems to come back to life.

"I like a good thriller. What's your last name? I'll look you up."

Shelly and I laugh, and Patrick looks irritated about being outside our inside joke.

"Shelly is my last name. It was Sheldon, but I changed it to Shelly since that's what everyone used to call me. Plus, Shelly looks better on the book covers. Levi is my first name."

"You're Levi Shelly?" Patrick asks, astonished at the man sitting before him.

"Um... yes." He looks almost embarrassed. This is the Shelly I remember.

"Holy shit, man. Your books are awesome! They've been made into movies! Blockbusters! You've sold millions of copies!"

Shelly lets out a quiet laugh. "Yes, I'm aware."

"You're Levi Shelly!" Patrick shouts out again, and I've noticed we've gained the attention of more than a few people. Good grief, this man is starstruck. I reach over and put my hand on Shelly's. "Don't mind him. He'll calm down soon."

Shelly's eyes twinkle with a smile as he covers my hand with his other one.

"I don't mind. I get to do what I love because I have fans like him... and you."

I return his smile before sliding my hand away and back to my lap. Shelly picks up his glass and drains the rest of the contents before setting it back down in front of him.

"Listen, I've got to run, but how about you come to my house tomorrow? I'm having a little cookout by the pool for some friends."

I look over to Patrick, and he's nodding his head yes. I laugh at his enthusiasm.

"It's a date!"

"Perfect, hand me your phone."

I give him my cell and watch as he adds himself as a contact. He punches the button to have my phone call his, and I hear his pocket ringing.

"If I don't save your number to know who's calling, I won't answer. Also, I need to text you my address. Noon tomorrow, and bring a swimsuit." He stands to leave, and I am sad to see him go. Our visit wasn't nearly long enough for as much catching up as I wanted to do.

I stand and hug him goodbye before he makes his way out the door. As I sit back down, I can't help but wonder what the odds are I would run into one of my dearest old friends at this random place. We were thick as thieves in college, and I've thought of him on and off through the years so many times.

We kept in touch for a while, and no one was more ecstatic than I was when his first book was a success. But time got in between us, and we lost touch. Speaking of time, it sure has treated him well. I don't remember him looking like that while we were in school. Shelly has turned into a major smoke show.

I look over to see if Patrick is ready to go.

"That was Levi Shelly," he says again. I laugh and shake my head at him. "You'll get to see him again tomorrow, babe. I promise."

5

"You look amazing," Patrick says as I walk out of the bathroom in my swimsuit. I head to the closet for the sundress I've chosen to wear over it.

"Thanks."

Patrick is relaxing on the bed when he clicks off the television and folds his arms behind his head. "Too bad you have to change."

I look down at the dress I've just pulled over my head, but I don't see any stains or holes.

"What do you mean?"

He gets up and walks over to me, taking my hands in his.

"I mean, there's no way I can let you walk into another man's house looking as sexy as you do in that little white bikini."

I blink up at him in confusion.

"Patrick, are you being sweet or chauvinistic right now? I can't tell."

He laughs under his breath. "Whichever one of those will get you to put on a different swimsuit that covers a little more of your fine-ass body is what I am right now. Just a little more—I'm not trying to set back the women's movement, but I also don't want to beat up every man with eyes who looks at you the way I know they're going to look at you."

I only brought one because I didn't believe we'd actually go swimming. I figured on the off chance we did, it would be the two of us at the hotel pool. That's why I packed my skimpiest, most scandalous string bikini—for Patrick.

However, even though circumstances have changed from what I originally intended when I packed it, I will never let a man tell me what I can or cannot wear, even if I do love him with all my heart. It seems I need to train him as to how to behave.

He starts to pull me in for a hug, but I put a hand on his chest to stop him. With the sweetest expression I can muster on my face, I tell him, "I am not responsible for men's thoughts or actions—they are. And, if you try to tell me what to wear or not wear again, I will walk in there as naked as the day I was born."

He laughs, but I don't.

"Now I can't tell if you're joking."

I raise an eyebrow at him to let him know I'm serious. "Try me."

He holds his hands up in surrender, but they move to cup my face as I pull him in for a kiss. After we break apart, he still holds my face in his hands, and he's looking at me like I'm the most precious thing in the world to him.

"Seriously, though. Were you and Levi Shelly a thing in college?"

With that question, he pops our intimate little bubble. Now we're getting into what he's actually worried about.

"A thing?" I know what he means, but I want him to ask me flat-out.

"Yeah, were you two an item, or did you ever hook up? I want to know what I'm walking into today."

I put my hands over his and meet his eyes so he will see the truth in my statement. "Shelly and I were best friends, nothing more and nothing less. Why do you ask? Are you jealous?"

Patrick looks insulted at my accusation. "I'm not jealous. I'm cautious."

"Do you trust me?" I echo his words from the restaurant back to him.

He puts a light kiss on my lips. "You, I trust. As for everyone else, not so much."

I shake my head at him to let him know how incorrigible I think he is. Patrick has a history of getting jealous in situations where he shouldn't, and this is one of them.

"Shelly is important to me even though I lost touch with him years ago. I was so excited when I saw him yesterday, and I hope we get a chance to catch up with each other today at the party. I meant what I said when I told you I wouldn't have been able to get through my Ph.D. program without him."

"So, he is just some friend from college?"

"Even though he has always been just a friend, you need to know he was a great friend. I told him all my secrets, and he told me his. He was there for me whenever I needed a shoulder to cry on with all the losers I dated and when my dad died. Hell, Shelly even crashed on my couch during his last semester of school because he couldn't afford his rent, and I was happy to help him. He means a lot to me, but I promise Shelly has never been more than a friend."

This seems to calm his fears enough that he doesn't try

to back out of us going to the cookout. We finish getting dressed and embark on finding Shelly's house, running only a half hour or so behind when we should have left.

"Do you have the address?" he asks as we walk out of our hotel.

"Yes, I forwarded Shelly's text to you before we left. We're heading back to the Garden District."

Patrick finds the text with the address Shelly sent to me earlier this morning. When he types it into his navigation app, he stops in his tracks. I get a few steps past him before I notice, and I have to walk back to where he has seemingly gone catatonic. I look over his shoulder to see what has his attention, but it's just a map. Patrick turns his head to look at me.

"Dawson, this man lives in the same neighborhood as Archie Manning."

I shrug because I'm not surprised by this at all. Shelly has done well for himself, and it couldn't have happened to a better person. Patrick shakes off his awed expression, and we start walking back to the streetcar.

Patrick double-checks the address before looking again at the house in front of us. "This is it."

I look up to see a jaw-dropping two-story home with wide columns, symmetrical windows, and iron railings on every balcony. It is the grandest house on the street with its white paint and black trim. It is old New Orleans at its finest, and it is breathtaking. We walk through the gate and admire the lush and exquisite landscaping as we make our way up the walk to ring the doorbell.

"This way, please," an older gentleman in full livery says

as he opens the door. We follow him through the house, and he leaves us as we exit through the back door. The party is in full swing, and we pause to take it all in.

Underneath the porch that runs the width of the house, there is a catered buffet. There are fancy-looking people milling about and socializing, grown men playing around in the enormous pool, and past that, there is a gazebo where a live band is stationed. Patrick and I send each other a look that says we're not in Kansas anymore. We don't make it three steps before Shelly is heading our way.

"I'm so glad you guys could make it."

"Just a little cookout with some friends?" I ask him as I gesture to the extravagant party happening in his backyard.

He looks sheepish. "I threw it all together at the last minute. It's not a big deal. When it's this hot outside, people flock to your house if you have a pool." He grabs my hand and helps me down the last few steps. "Please help yourselves to the buffet, and there is an open bar to the right, past the pool."

"I'm on it. What do you want to drink, Dawson?" Patrick asks.

"You're my favorite bartender, so surprise me."

Patrick nods and heads toward the bar, and Shelly leads me to a couple of unoccupied lounge chairs.

"Did you put on sunscreen?" he asks before we stretch out under the intense sun. He takes off his t-shirt, and I notice his upper body is toned and tanned. He's got some ink on the lower part of his abdomen, but I don't get a chance to look closely enough to find out what it is. What did he ask me about? Oh, sunscreen.

"Yes. I applied copious amounts of it before I left the hotel."

"That's too bad," I hear him say under his breath. I'm

about to ask what he meant by that when Patrick strolls back up to us and hands me a tall plastic cup.

"It's a Pimm's cup. You're going to love it."

I take a sip, and he's right. It's good. "Thanks. This is awesome."

"No problem. So, listen. I know we just got here, but would you mind if I left you? I mean, there are Saints in the pool."

"What?" I ask, laughing. "I had no idea you were religious."

Patrick takes off his shirt and shakes his head. "No, like there are real New Orleans Saints players in the pool playing volleyball. This is a bucket list situation. So, are you cool if I just..." he points both thumbs over his shoulder and nods his head toward the game he's dying to get in on.

"Go with God," I say with a sarcastic bow of my head mere seconds before I hear the sound the water makes as his body splashes into the pool.

"You've done well for yourself, Shel." I look over his backyard and notice a few celebrities, one or two models, and a handful of politicians besides the professional athletes who are in the pool with Patrick. All these people of untold wealth, beauty, or influence, and he chooses to lie here and talk with me. That's my sweet Shelly.

"Yeah, I'm a bit better off now than the last time you saw me." He says this with a self-deprecating tone—in what has to be the understatement of the century. I nod at the truth in his words. The last time I saw him, he didn't have two nickels to rub together.

Shelly's eyes steer away from mine, and I hope it's not from embarrassment.

"None of that ever mattered to me. You know that, don't

you?" I reach out and touch his hand, drawing him back to me.

"I know. I wouldn't be where I am today if it weren't for you. I know that sounds cliché, but it's the truth. Your help and friendship came at a pivotal point in my life, and I owe it all to you. I wouldn't have made it without you, Dawson."

I scoff at the idea. "Oh, please. You'd have made it to where you are with or without my help. All this success? This is all you." I wave my hand to gesture again at our grand surroundings.

"It's not all it's cracked up to be. Sometimes, I'd give anything to go back to sitting on your little apartment's fire escape, watching the stars, and eating crappy food."

"And philosophizing about all of life," I add.

"Exactly." He gives me half a smile.

I take another sip of my drink, but it does little to cool me off. I am hesitant to showcase my little-to-nothing swimsuit, but it's too hot to keep on this dress if we're going to lie here under the sun. I stand to take it off and pull the dress over my head in one swoop.

"God damn."

I look over at Shelly with a puzzled expression before draping the dress over the top of the lounge. He meets my stare with a smile, daring me to ask.

"Excuse me?" I laugh because I can't believe my shy Shelly said what I think he did. I sit back down on my chair, and he shifts to lie on his side toward me, looking intense and unapologetic.

"I said, 'God damn'. I said God damn because there is no other reaction any red-blooded male can have to you looking the way you do but that—God damn."

He says the words slower this time as his eyes take their time in making another pass over my body.

"Thank you?" I laugh off the awkwardness. Shelly turns to lie on his back again, and we continue to bake away under the sun's rays.

"I'm glad you got rid of Mack."

I forgot how much I love his frankness. I would say I was grateful for the change of subject, but changing that subject to my ex-husband isn't the direction I wanted to go.

"You warned me about him. I should have listened." I shrug, even though he won't see it. Shelly hated Mack from the first moment they met, like how dogs can sense evil.

"I did warn you—several times. I even warned you right before you got on the back of his motorcycle and drove out of my life after graduation. You married him, didn't you?"

"Yeah. Our divorce was final earlier this year. I've been dating Patrick since right before the divorce." I look over at Shelly, and he's looking back at me.

"No time for self-discovery in between?"

I shake my head at him. "What's left to discover? I'm thirty years old and a professor of literature at Bellhurst College. I'm practically an old schoolmarm."

He shakes his head back at me. "Not looking like that, you're not. Do you still write?"

I laugh at his question. "Oh, I was never a serious writer. Not like you."

He stares at me for a moment.

"So, you've stopped writing."

I wave off the judgment I hear in his comment. "That silly little novel I was playing around with when we were in school pales in comparison to what you write. I'm surprised you even remember it."

He laughs to himself like I'm not in on the joke.

"Had enough of this heat yet?" he asks. I look down and

notice I've almost finished my drink, and I am turning a little pink.

"Yeah, I wouldn't mind hanging out in the shade for a few."

"I'd love to give you a tour of the place if you'd like. It's on the historical registry, and it's a pretty awesome house if I do say so myself."

I look over at Patrick and see he's having the time of his life in the pool, so I don't see what it could hurt.

"I'll admit, I wanted to run through your place and look at everything as soon as your servant guy let us in."

Shelly laughs at my comment. "I don't have a servant guy. I have wait staff I've hired for the day, but no servant guy. Besides, I'm usually here by myself."

"All alone?"

"I do have the occasional guest now and then." He winks at me, and I catch his meaning. I guess Shelly is a regular playboy these days. That's one bet I would have never taken in college.

"Oh, um... good for you. I bet you date a lot, don't you?"

He shrugs. "Compared to when we were in school, any dating would be considered a lot. I do okay. It's never boring in this city, that's for sure. So, how about that tour?"

"I would love that, but I would love anything that came with air conditioning right now."

Shelly gets up first and wraps a towel around his waist before taking my hand to help me get up from my lounge chair. He doesn't step back right away when I stand, which puts my body less than an inch from his.

He looks at me for a moment before stepping away, but that look is causing problems. I know that look. I've made that look. That look has intentions and an agenda. I haven't been around him in years, but I could swear what has been going on since I got here is more than innocent banter between friends.

I can't be imagining what all these looks and comments he's made today mean. This man is coming on to me, which is just plain weird. In all the years we were around each other in college, he never made a pass at me. Not one. He even lived in my apartment! There were times I wasn't so sure we didn't play for the same team, but now I have little doubt he's on the opposite side of the field from me.

I reach for my sundress to slip back over my head, and it causes him to frown.

"Look, Shel. I don't know if it's a good idea for me to take a tour right now. I'll just grab a plate of food and sit in the shade over there instead." I point to where most people have congregated to get out of the heat.

Shelly looks down at his feet before bringing his eyes back to meet mine. In that one move, he changed from the grown man who was coming on to me back into the boy I used to be friends with.

"I'm sorry, Dawson. I didn't mean to make you uncomfortable. In my defense, you weren't playing fair with that bikini," he laughs at his own joke, "but I didn't mean to make this awkward. I've missed you, and I want to catch up. I'll be good. I promise." He takes his hand and makes a cross over his heart with his finger.

The sun beats down on the top of my head while I take a moment to decide. Maybe I'm making a big deal out of nothing. He seems sincere in his apology for the unease he has created between us, and he's giving me the opportunity to see his gorgeous home. Oh, what the hell.

"It would save me from a heat stroke," I say as I give in and head toward the back door.

Once we get inside, I let him take the lead since he's the

one giving the tour. I see he doesn't have his towel anymore. He must have discarded it before we got in the house. I also notice he hasn't put his shirt back on as I follow him to the kitchen, and I watch the muscles in his back move as he walks in front of me. It's obvious he works out regularly, which is something the Shelly I knew never did. His new dedication to exercise sure is paying off.

The wait staff is bustling in and out of the kitchen, so we don't stay long. Next are the dining and living rooms, and then we head up the stairs. He is telling me the history of the place as we go from room to room. It was built in the 1830s, and when he bought it, it hadn't had a major renovation in over fifty years.

"You did a great job blending the old with the new. I can't imagine how long this took you."

"I'm a patient man," he says as we reach the second-floor landing. "Now I'll show you where all the magic happens." He laughs as he says this, and I figure we're heading into the main bedroom.

He walks inside and turns to look at me, but I've stopped right after walking through the door. He moves to prop his forearm on one of his antique bed posts while he waits for me to take in the room.

"It's beautiful." My eyes wander all around the large room. The dark navy and cream color scheme is sophisticated yet masculine, much like Shelly is now.

I look at the man standing in the middle of his bedroom, and I have to admit--he is beautiful as well. In all the years I've known him, I never pictured him like this, as the virile, sexual hunk of a man who is now standing before me in his bedroom, scanning me with his eyes.

I can't help but glance at his broad chest and ripped abs because I'm only human. Immediate guilt hits me for the images that flit through my mind and the thoughts that trail after them. I'm about to look away when I recognize his tattoo.

"Wait a minute. Is that...?" I'm walking toward him, and I reach out for his lower abdomen before I realize what I'm doing and pull my hand back.

"Maybe," is all he says.

His black swim shorts hang low on his hips, and his tattoo looks almost tribal. The blue ink starts underneath the waistline—where I can't see it—but I can see the wings that come up to end on both sides of his navel.

Except the wings aren't made of feathers.

"Ivy. The wings are made of ivy. Is your tattoo..."

I shake my head before I finish my question. There is no way this is what I think it is.

"Ask me."

His eyes are intense as he stares at me. I look at him, trying to ferret out the answer without asking the question, but I have to know.

"Is your tattoo... is it from my novel? The wings are made of ivy. Is there a crescent moon between them?"

His smile looks downright dangerous before he asks, "Want to see?"

I do want to see it since my brain created it, but when his hand slides down to the button holding up his shorts, I decide this isn't the best idea.

"You promised you'd be good," I remind him.

He walks toward me like he's on the prowl.

"You've never liked good. Only the bad boys ever held your attention."

I start to walk backward out of the room.

"I'm kidding," he says, laughing and holding his hands up in a placating gesture as if the spell he was under had been broken. "Yes, it's from your story. Your story inspired me to become a writer."

I shake my head in disbelief, both at the notion that I had anything to do with his prolific writing career or that he memorialized my story on his body in such a permanent way. Shelly sees my stunned expression and laughs.

"I thought I'd be an English professor, and you'd be the famous author. Ironic how it all worked out, but I want you to know your story meant everything to me. You meant everything to me. That's why I got the tattoo."

In a slow movement, he runs his hands over his lower abdomen, and my eyes follow. I let out a long breath, which I didn't know I was holding in.

He sees he's gotten my attention. "It's pretty wicked if I do say so myself. Now, if you can restrain yourself, I'll pull my shorts down just enough for you to see it. Don't go crazy on me, though." He laughs, but he waits for my reaction before following through. That tells me the old Shelly is still there, and I can trust him not to get out of hand. At least, that is how I rationalize my desire to look at a tattoo based on a story I wrote, even though it happens to be down a gorgeous guy's pants.

"Uh-huh. No worries. I can control myself, and I do want to look at it, so…" I snap my fingers, indicating to him he should hurry up so we can get this over with.

He gives me a naughty grin, but he is true to his word as he pulls his shorts down just to the point where I can see the waxing crescent moon. It is pretty wicked and so detailed. I bend down to see the tiny arrows coming off the tips of the moon when I hear, "Do you guys need a minute? I'd say, 'Get a room,' but it looks like you've already found one."

Oh, shit.

6

The look on Patrick's face when I turn around is one I hope to never see again for the rest of my life. Hurt, betrayal, and anger all play out on his features at the same time. He rushes down the stairs before I replay in my head what he must have seen when he came into the room, and my heart breaks. How do I explain the sequence of events that led my face to be three inches from a man's crotch in a secluded bedroom away from the rest of the partygoers?

"Patrick!" I shout from the top of the stairs as I watch him leave through the front door, slamming it behind him. I start to run after him, but Shelly reaches out to grab my arm before I can get down the staircase.

"Wait. Don't go." His eyes are pleading with me.

I look down at his hand, holding my arm, and back at him before jerking it away.

"Of course, I'm leaving! Patrick thinks we were doing something we were not doing, and I have to explain!" I get halfway down the stairs before I come to a sudden stop.

"Shit."

Pour Boy

Shelly jogs down to where I am, looking concerned.

"What is it?"

"I didn't bring my purse. I left it since I would be with Patrick all day, and he could keep anything I needed in his pockets. I don't even have my phone. I can't get back to the hotel!"

I'm freaking out. I don't know the way back. Patrick will think I chose not to come after him and explain. He's going to believe the worst because that's what he thinks he saw.

I put my hands in my hair and start to pull, but Shelly grabs them and brings them back down.

"It's okay. Tell me where you're staying, and I'll take you there. Just give me a minute to say goodbye to some guests and tell the staff."

"Yes, please hurry!" I tell him before shuffling him down the rest of the stairs.

Shelly does his best, but it is still a good fifteen minutes before we are in his garage and ready to leave. He has to move a few notebooks and random pieces of paper into the backseat of his luxury sedan before I sit down, and once I get in, I notice the cup holders are full of empty stainless-steel coffee tumblers. It is the opposite experience of riding in Patrick's vehicle, and it makes me miss him even more and regret putting our relationship in jeopardy over stupid, careless actions.

About a block from the hotel, I see Patrick. I guess riding the streetcars makes for slower travel. I point him out to Shelly, and he pulls the car over. I jump out before he has it in park and run to Patrick.

"It wasn't what it looked like!" I say before he sees me. His eyes are red, and it looks like he's been crying. It breaks my heart all over again. I love this man fiercely, and I know what he saw hurt him. Patrick looks at me and seems like he wants to talk until he notices who is standing behind me.

His face shuts down. "Why is he here?" he asks in a deadly whisper.

"He offered to drive me back to our hotel."

Patrick's hands are balled into fists at his side when he abruptly turns and walks away from me.

I try to spin him back around, wanting him to talk to me, but he won't budge.

"I didn't have my phone or my..."

"Just go. Walk away. I need you to not be where I am right now, Dawson."

He picks up his speed, and I'm too stunned and hurt to follow him. Why wouldn't he let me explain?

Shelly comes up to stand beside me. "Sorry. I should have driven off, but I wanted to be sure you were okay. He seemed pretty mad."

"Ya think?" I ask in my best sarcastic tone.

"Let's get you to your room so you can get your phone. I'm sure he'll cool down and want to talk."

"That's a great idea except for one thing. My room key is in the hotel room—with my wallet and identification. The room is in Patrick's name, so I doubt it would help even if I did have my ID on me. Without Patrick here, there's no way I can get back in."

Shelly puts a finger to his lip as he contemplates the situation for a moment.

"I can fix this," he says as he pulls out his phone and walks a few steps away. He makes two more calls in quick succession before walking back to where I'm standing. Without telling me what happened, he leads me to his car and opens the door for me.

"Well?" I ask as I get into the passenger's seat.

"It's done."

"What's done?" I try to ask before he tucks me inside and shuts the door. He won't give me any more information on our short ride to the French Royal Inn. A valet opens his door, and one is right behind him to open mine.

"Mr. Shelly! We're so glad to have you at our hotel this evening," the valet says as we exit the vehicle.

"Mr. Shelly, welcome!" a well-dressed older gentleman says as soon as he clears the hotel's front door. He meets us on the sidewalk and shakes Shelly's hand.

"Thank you very much for your help with our little predicament," Shelly says to who I assume is the hotel manager.

"Oh, it's no trouble at all." The mystery man waves away even the slightest possibility of imposition. We go to the front desk, and an over-eager receptionist presents us with two room keys to mine and Patrick's room. Shelly gets directions to the room from her even though he could have asked me, and he puts a hand on my back to lead me in its direction. We make it to the courtyard before I say my first words.

"How did you do that?"

Shelly shrugs and tries to play it off. "My charming personality?"

"Nope, not buying it."

He laughs. "Southern hospitality?"

I shake my head, but now I'm laughing at him.

"Nope. Try again."

"The promise to hold my next book launch party at this fine establishment?"

I stop in my tracks and spin around to look at him.

"You did that just so I could get back into my hotel room?"

"Dawson, my dear. We all have to work with what we've

got. Despite what I write in my novels, I'm rubbish at picking locks. You needed to get back into your room, and I had a way to make it happen."

I reach up and hug him.

"Thank you. For real, thank you, but you shouldn't have done it."

He puts his hands on my shoulders and looks into my eyes.

"I couldn't leave you to sit on the stoop and wait for that angry man to find it in his heart to come back. I couldn't leave you stranded."

I want to argue with him, but he's right. I would have been stranded with no money and no phone. I want to think Patrick didn't realize the situation he was leaving me in, but the point is—he should have.

"Thank you," I say again as I squeeze his hand. I continue heading to my room, and I can't help but notice Shelly is still following me. I don't want him to get the wrong idea in letting him follow me to my room, but I also don't want him to feel like I'm dismissing him after he gave so much for me to be able to get back inside of it.

I stop him at the door. "Let me slip in and get my stuff. Then, if you have time, I'd like it if we walked around for a bit."

"Walk around so you can look for Patrick?" He has always been too smart for his own good.

"Maybe," I say with a shrug.

"And if we don't find him, can we maybe grab dinner together?"

As soon as he mentions dinner, I realize this is another day I've let breakfast and lunch go by without anything to eat. I never made it to the cookout part of Shelly's cookout.

"If we don't find him, then yes. We can grab a quick bite somewhere."

"Perfect."

I pop into my room and grab my purse, put my phone inside it, and double-check that I have my wallet. Shelly is waiting at the door when I come out.

"Thank you so much for helping me look for Patrick. I know this isn't how you planned to spend your day."

He props his arm on the door frame and leans into me. "Any day I get to spend with you is a good day."

We walk back through the courtyard to the hotel's exit. When we make it to the street, I glance up at him. "Do you have any idea where to start?"

Shelly holds up his hands. "He could be anywhere. I don't know him, and you aren't familiar with the city. We're looking for a needle in a haystack, which, by the way, is much better than looking for a hay in a needle stack."

I laugh at his stupid joke. This is the old Shelly, trying to make me feel better when a guy makes me sad.

7

We walk for hours. I see every inch of The French Quarter twice but don't find Patrick. Shelly never complains. He even has me show him a picture of him a time or two to refresh his memory of what Patrick looks like before heading into another bar to try to find my long-lost boyfriend.

When we watch the sun set behind the buildings, I call it. I'm tired, hungry, and pissed. Patrick isn't answering my calls or texts and is nowhere to be found.

"Please feed me," I say to Shelly as I come out of the last dive I'm going to look inside of for someone who doesn't want to be found.

"Words I've been longing to hear. Let's go." Shelly leads me a few blocks to a little restaurant hidden away down a side street.

Before we go in, I look down at my sundress and sandals. "Do I look alright for this place?" I ask, not knowing what kind of upscale establishments he frequents.

His eyes roam over me once more before he moves to stand right in front of me. He puts a hand on my waist. His other hand wraps a strand of my hair loosely around his finger before he drops it back into place.

"Dawson, you look more than alright." He looks at my mouth before shaking himself out of his thoughts and stepping back. He looks like he wanted to say more but stopped himself.

"But you shouldn't worry about this place. If you want fancy, I can show you fancy. However, if you want the best po'boy and gumbo you will ever eat in your natural-born life, it's right through that door."

When I walk inside, I notice two things. One, this place is a pretty laid-back restaurant. No one is in a ball gown or cocktail dress, so that's a plus. The second thing I notice is it's packed to the gills.

Shelly walks up and speaks to the hostess. He slips her what I'm assuming is a wad of cash, and her eyes widen when she recognizes him. In less than two minutes, we are headed to our table near the back of the restaurant in a secluded alcove.

I don't let myself make eye contact with all the people we pass who are still waiting for their tables. It's not my fault they didn't have the foresight to bring a worldwide bestselling author to dinner with them tonight.

A buxom blonde waitress saunters up to our table, and it takes everything I have not to roll my eyes. Here we go again. Where do New Orleans restaurants get their wait staff? Frederick's of Hollywood? The Hustler Club?

She takes a lighter out of her pocket and lights the candle I didn't notice sitting on our table. She hands me a menu before almost turning her back to me and handing Shelly his. This time, I do roll my eyes, and Shelly sees it. He laughs under his breath at me.

Shelly moves his attention back to the waitress and cuts

her off mid-sentence, ending what I'm sure was a practiced sales pitch—although what she was trying to sell to him is probably up for debate. Her body language suggests it's more than food she has to offer.

"Please, if you don't mind, I'd rather you tell my date the specials. She's never been to your restaurant before."

Date? I raise my eyebrows, and he shakes his head discreetly, wanting me to let it go. Bimbo Barbie turns to me, and I listen to the night's specials and smile at our waitress until she walks away from the table. As soon as she is out of earshot, my smile slips off my face like it was held on by grease.

"Date?"

He laughs at my sudden change in demeanor and shrugs his shoulders. "It was the easiest way to let her know she doesn't have a chance in hell with me. I didn't mean to make you uncomfortable."

"Yeah, I guess I can see your point. I was waiting for her to crawl onto your lap."

I'm being overly sensitive, and I've got to stop doing that. Shelly has been nothing but a perfect gentleman all evening and has taken care of me when someone else left me high and dry. If he refers to me as his date to get a waitress off his back, so be it.

When she returns, I get a kick out of ordering for both of us while Shelly doesn't give her any attention. She pouts a little as she walks away, and I almost feel sorry for her.

"She's pretty if you like that hourglass figure and perfect skin sort of thing." I fake a shiver and make a face to pretend she grosses me out.

"If she thinks she can compete with you, she needs to buy a better mirror."

"You're sweet," I say, playing off his compliment.

Pour Boy

"I'm not as sweet as I used to be."

I ignore what he could mean by that loaded comment and change the subject. He graciously lets me, but that look never leaves his eyes.

When our dinner arrives, I am blown away. Shelly is right about it being the best po'boy I've ever tasted. It doesn't matter if it's the only one I've ever tasted. I'm one hundred percent sure it can't get better than this.

"This sucker is difficult to eat," I tell him after I've tried everything except unhinging my jaw to fit the tall sandwich in for another bite—so much for a ladylike appearance.

"You've got a little..." He points to my cheek.

"What?" I put my hand up to where he was pointing but don't feel anything.

"Some remoulade... just... there," he says, rubbing it off my cheek with his thumb. "Got it."

I feel tingles where he touched my cheek, and those tingles zip to all the wrong places in my body, making them feel very right. My lips part as I watch him take his thumb and put it in his mouth to suck off the sauce while never breaking eye contact with me. I know a dare when I see one.

I put my hands in my lap and break my staring contest with Shelly. "Why are you doing this?" I all but whisper, still looking down at my hands.

"Doing what?"

I guess he's going to make me walk right up to the elephant in the room and introduce myself.

I glance back up at him. Was I blind in college, or was he not as gorgeous as he is now, sitting across this table from me? He's looking at me like he wants me for dinner, and although he is hot and his attention is flattering, this shouldn't be happening. I know Patrick and I are having a rough go of it at the moment, but that does not change my deep love for him.

I can admit I'm attracted to Shelly. I never was before, but the man he has become is sexy as hell—there's no denying that. However, he's no match for Patrick where my heart is concerned. Shelly will always know the girl I used to be, but Patrick knows who I am now—the woman I've put my blood, sweat, and tears into creating. The woman he has helped me create.

I like who I am now, and I love how Patrick goes out of his way to appreciate me and show me how important I am to him. What we have is real, and real doesn't always mean pretty. I know he misunderstood what he saw, and it made him mad and jealous. I don't understand why he walked away, but I will hear him out when he's ready. Patrick means the world to me, and I won't sacrifice our relationship because my old friend from college has had a glow-up. I'll fight for what Patrick and I have because it's rare and wonderful, even if it means being direct with Shelly on his behavior and recognizing my own. I want to be able to have dinner with my old friend without feeling like I'm playing with fire.

"Why are you hitting on me?"

There's no sense in beating around the bush. It's time to call a spade a spade. "You've made little moves all day, and it doesn't make sense. So yeah, I'm calling you out. In all the years I've known you, you've been my friend and nothing more. You know I'm with Patrick. Why are you hitting on me now when I've found my place in life? When I'm finally happy?"

Shelly sits up straighter and leans forward in his chair.

"Are you? Are you happy? Have you found your place in life? Because there seems to be a whole other Dawson you've left behind. The one who has roamed the city streets all day looking for someone who stranded her in an unfamiliar city... she doesn't seem all that happy."

I hate to admit how valid his points are, but I won't concede them. He doesn't understand, but maybe I don't either. I'll start with the argument that's easier to win since Patrick's actions are currently unexplainable.

"What do you mean I've 'left a Dawson behind'? I know who I am now more than I ever have before. I've been through hell and back in the last year, and it has made me stronger. I like who I've become. You haven't had the chance to get to know who I am now. You only know the idealistic college girl who thought she had some talent in writing."

His eyes bug out of his head.

"Thought she had some talent? Are you kidding? I have an entire tattoo that would argue against everything you just said. Dawson, you are a phenomenal writer, but you have been too much of a coward to push yourself—to put yourself out there—to make yourself vulnerable."

I can't help but be offended at what Shelly is saying to me. "Don't look down from your best-seller status and lecture me about not writing. I'm fine without it, and it's not like I'd have your success, anyway. I can't be the girl you've created in your head over the years, Shelly. That is the Dawson that doesn't exist. Vulnerability has nothing to do with it."

He shakes his head, and his passion for this subject lights up his eyes.

"Baby, vulnerability has everything to do with it. I wish I could convince you to try because there's no other feeling like it. Well—maybe one—but Dawson, I want to see you lay yourself bare. Be vulnerable enough to let people read what's inside of you and give them the power to judge you...

to like, love, or hate you. It takes guts and nerves of steel, but you said you're stronger now. Prove it. Stop being a coward and go back to writing. Put it out into the world. You're hiding the best part of yourself because I know that's where you shine. That is where you belong, stripped down to your soul."

I sit back in my chair with the force of his words. Damn, he is a good writer, but what he's saying isn't fiction. He's right. I did leave a piece of myself along the way. It was a dream I buried underneath a mountain of doubt and attempts to please other people. I sacrificed more than I thought I did for my ex-husband. Patrick has brought light and happiness into my life since he stepped into it, but there are some things I still need to do for myself.

"I do miss it. I miss how real it made me feel, even though I was creating worlds that don't exist."

"That's because it's who you are. Stop turning your back on that part of yourself. No matter what you decide to do about the Neanderthal you're dating now, whether you go back with him or abandon all your earthly possessions and stay here with me, promise me you'll write again."

There's a lot to unpack in what he's said, and I'm not sure where to start. Is that what he's thinking about? Does he believe me staying here with him is even an option?

"Patrick is not a Neanderthal. He is truly a great guy, and I hate you didn't get to find that out for yourself. This is the first real fight we've ever had, and you have to admit, what he saw was pretty incriminating."

He takes a sip of the Sazerac I ordered for him and sets it back on the table. "He does have great taste in books. I can give him that much, but I only want the best for you. You're my girl."

"Shel, you knew me better than anyone a long time ago,

but you haven't seen how much I've changed. I no longer let people in my life who are bad for me. You're going off the person I was in college, and I wouldn't trust her either where boyfriends are concerned. However, Patrick is the real deal. What we have is special, and I would have reacted a lot worse had I walked in on Patrick like he did us."

He sits with what I said for a moment and thinks about it. "But you're not writing. To me, that means you're not where you need to be."

"I see where you're coming from." I lean toward him and place my hand on his. "I am still healing from what Mack put me through, and I did lose a piece of myself along the way. I'm getting there, and I'm stronger every day. I promise I will try to write again, but that's as far as my promise goes. I'll try it on to see if it still fits."

"That's my girl." He smiles like he couldn't be prouder. "You know, New Orleans has been known to inspire a writer or two. You could stay the rest of the summer. I'd be happy to drive you back before the fall semester starts."

I narrow my eyes at him. "That is the second time you've mentioned me staying down here. See, this is you doing that thing again."

He chuckles once and shakes his head as he leans back in his chair, tossing his napkin on the table.

"Not very well, apparently."

"Levi Sheldon. What in the hell are you trying to accomplish? Please don't ruin our friendship with your new testosterone-laden libido. I just found you again, and that would suck."

The waitress chooses this moment to walk up and present the bill, and we both pretend she didn't hear what I said. I reach for the purse I'd plucked from my room, but

Shelly has some cash in the waitress's hand before I can pull out my wallet.

"Thank you," I say as he leads us from the table to the door.

"I'm happy to do it." I hear the truth in his words. In college, he had trouble feeding himself, much less buying both of us a nice meal. I smile, knowing he'll never have to worry about things like that again.

We head back into the warm night air toward the hotel. We're just a few blocks away, which is wild considering all the streets we've walked up and down today.

He takes me to my hotel room, and I don't argue. I've made it as clear as I can that nothing can happen between us, and selfishly, I'd rather not be alone. I don't think Patrick would take off back to Starkford without me, but I never thought he'd leave me like he did today.

Shelly hangs back as I open the door and peer inside. My disappointment Patrick isn't inside the room is obvious. My shoulders sag out of sheer hopelessness. Did I ruin the wonderful thing we had so easily? Could I not have the benefit of the doubt even once?

I turn to Shelly to tell him he should go, but he can guess what I'm about to say before I say it.

"No way in hell am I leaving you alone right now." He turns me around in that gentle way of his and steers me deeper into the room, letting the door close behind him.

I walk to the bed and lie down on top of the covers. I roll my face into the pillow to muffle my scream of frustration so we don't get a SWAT team in here trying to find out who was murdered. Tears start to stream out of my eyes, and there's nothing I can do to stop them. The day has finally caught up with me.

The bed dips on the other side, and Shelly's hand comes to rest on my back, rubbing small circles.

"He doesn't deserve you."

I wipe the tears away from under my eyes as I turn on my side to face him.

"Yes, he does. There's got to be a reasonable explanation for this. I know Patrick, and he wouldn't hurt me like this."

Shelly rolls his eyes at my optimism. "There is no good reason for leaving you like he did, without the chance to explain. It's been hours, and you haven't heard a word from him."

"I know."

He lets out a deep sigh and takes my hand in his. Instead of holding it, he threads his fingers between mine in a slow, comforting rhythm.

"I planned to come back for you."

That takes my attention away from our hands and back to his earnest-looking face.

"What?"

"After I made something of myself. You said I never hit on you in all the years we were friends. I wanted to. Every day, I wanted to, but I had nothing to offer you. You liked flashy guys with motorcycles, and I couldn't even afford a ten-speed bike."

"Shelly—"

He cuts me off. "No. I loved you from the start, but I'm smart. I knew you weren't ready to love me back the way I wanted, so I settled for what I could get. Settled isn't the right word because our friendship meant the world to me, but I'd be lying if I said I never hoped it could be more. I think about you every day, every time I take off my clothes and see my tattoo."

"You shouldn't be saying these things to me. You're my friend, and I love you so much."

"I knew you didn't see me as anything more than a friend, but Dawson, I had a plan. I've just made it to where I wanted to be in my career. Now I have something to offer you. I was about to find you and convince you to run away with me. I'd even get us a motorcycle to ride into the sunset on if that's what it would take to get you to be with me."

I shake my head back and forth.

"I never knew."

"Because I never wanted you to know. But now I can offer you the world. I can give you everything you've ever wanted."

Another tear falls down my cheek.

He doesn't understand. He's always been so smart in some ways, but in others, he doesn't get it.

"No, you can't. I wish you could, but you can't because what I want more than anything is Patrick. I love him. I love him with all my heart, and even though I can't explain what he did today, I know he loves me, too. That's why I ran after him. That's why I looked for him. It's because I'll always look for him. I don't want to hurt you. I love you so much, but I love you as a friend."

His shoulders slump as I say the word friend, and I feel like I've stuck a knife in his back. I haven't been a good friend through the years. I haven't kept up with him, haven't nurtured our friendship in any way, and now when he confesses how he has loved me all this time—I hurt him.

"Shel, it's been years since I've seen you. Now that we've found each other again, I don't want to lose you from my life, but it seems cruel to ask you to stay knowing what you want from me is different than what I want from you. I don't know what to do."

He's quiet for a moment as his hand plays with mine.

"Do you want me in your life as a friend, even though you know I'll always want it to be more?"

I am about to respond to his question, but I realize I'm not the one who can answer it. "It depends. Can you be in my life knowing I've given my heart, one hundred percent of it, to Patrick?"

He picks up my hand and brings it to his lips, giving it a light kiss.

He seems to take a moment to think about it before he sighs again. "I'll be whatever you need me to be. Whatever I can have of you, I will take."

"Can you be happy?"

He gives me a self-deprecating chuckle. "I don't know about happiness, but I believe I'll be less unhappy with you in my life even if I'm friend-zoned. Again."

I laugh, and it makes him laugh a little despite himself.

I squeeze his hand. "That would make me less unhappy, too."

8

It's late, and I'm tired. I shouldn't have drifted off to sleep in my hotel bed with a man who is not my boyfriend lying next to me, but I did.

It doesn't matter because Patrick hasn't come back. My soul must miss him because I dream about him.

It is one of those dreams in which the scenes keep changing. At first, I'm back at the top of Shelly's staircase, yelling for Patrick to stop. When he doesn't, I put my fingers in my mouth and let out a loud whistle, which is something I've never been able to do in real life.

In full uniform, The New Orleans Saints football team rushes from the pool and out the front door, grabbing Patrick as he tries to escape. They carry him on their shoulders back into the house and deposit him at my feet. The foyer and half the living room are filled with wet Saints players glaring at him menacingly and daring him to move.

Because he can't leave, I am allowed the time to explain what happened. Patrick understands, and we go out back to play volleyball in the pool. Patrick and I are even given honorary uniforms to wear, helmets and all.

Pour Boy

In the next scene, I am a Voodoo priestess under a waxing crescent moon. My hair is jet black and tied in a messy bun on top of my head. My dress is little more than a black rag, tattered and torn in several places. I slaved away all night in this old New Orleans cemetery until I had the right incantation to bring Patrick back to me.

I make a clockwise circle of white candles to surround me and my work area, going over and on top of several graves. I place a yellow candle at the correct spot to mark the direction of east. At the opposite end, a blue candle marks west. A red one marks south, and I place a green candle on its opposing side to mark north. I walk in a clockwise path, envisioning the color of each direction in my mind's eye as I move toward it, chanting the spell I am weaving into existence.

The sky becomes violent with claps of thunder and bolts of lightning, but it holds back its rain. Worry I will never find my long-lost love tries to inch its way into my thoughts, but I hold firm to my vision. The atmosphere is proof of the crescendo building inside me, and I've never felt more powerful.

Electricity wicks itself from the ground and into my feet. It travels up my body in hammering pulses. Sweat rolls from my brow, and my breathing becomes labored. With a mighty roll of thunder, the heavens open, and rain pours down. The sheets of rain that fall extinguish my candles in a counterclockwise pattern, and I know my prayer has been heard.

Moments later, Patrick appears through the fog and walks toward me until he can wrap me in his arms. We make love under the stars in the middle of the circle until we're too exhausted to move.

The next scene lacks the pizzazz of my earlier dreams.

I'm in a dark room and hear a door open, followed by Patrick's voice.

"You have got to be fucking kidding me."

"It's not what you think," says a sleepy voice that sounds like Shelly.

"Why does everyone keep telling me that today." Patrick sounds closer than he was before.

The bed moves, and I realize it's Shelly getting up.

Oh, God. This isn't a dream.

"Why did you leave her without letting her explain what happened? She's been a wreck all day because of you," Shelly whispers, not knowing I'm awake.

A wreck? I don't know if I'd use the word 'wreck.' I wasn't that bad—okay, maybe I was. I decide to keep my eyes shut a little longer and get the lay of the land before charging into battle with Patrick.

"I didn't get but a block away when I realized Dawson was trying to tell me she didn't have her wallet or room key on her."

"Or her phone," Shelly snips.

"Well, that makes two of us. I forgot I had my phone in my pocket when I jumped into your pool earlier today. When I climbed up the stairs at your house, I was looking for Dawson to let her know I had drowned my phone. It's completely broken. That's when I saw—whatever the hell it was I saw you two doing in your bedroom."

"That explains why you didn't answer her calls, but why didn't you come back to the hotel?"

"I did!" Patrick whisper-shouts. "I came right back, and I must have only missed you two by ten minutes at the most. I asked the receptionist, and she said you and Dawson had just left. I searched and searched, but I couldn't find her anywhere. I spent the rest of the day looking for her, and I came back here several times to check with the receptionist to see if she'd come back. I even went to your house."

"I didn't get a call." I can hear the shrug in Shelly's voice.

"They weren't super helpful. No one would give me your number or let me use your phone, and I was asked in a not-so-polite manner to leave the premises. When I got back to the hotel, the receptionist said Dawson came back, but when I got to my room, my key didn't work. I went to the front desk, and it seems my reservation is in your name now. If I hadn't threatened them with every type of lawsuit under the sun, they would have never given me a new key to my own room! So, please tell me, how the hell is this even possible?"

The seething in Patrick's voice is evident. I might be a coward because I wait for Shelly to respond.

"You left her without her phone, her driver's license, and her wallet... What was I supposed to do? She needed to get back into her room, so I made it happen."

"Is that all you made happen?" Patrick asks as both a warning and a threat.

"Unfortunately."

Dear baby Jesus, tell me Shelly did not just say that. My eyes pop open, but neither of them seems to notice. They probably can't see me through the thick cloud of testosterone in the air.

"Boy, do you have a death wish?" Patrick appears in my peripheral vision. He's speaking at full volume now, and he looks like he's ready to throw Shelly through the window. I close my eyes again, deciding to be a coward a little longer.

"Calm down, Bruce Banner, and I'm not your boy. You'll be happy to know we decided to be just friends."

Patrick lets out a sharp laugh. "We?"

"Well, more like "she," but you need to understand—I

do plan to be her friend. Having a problem with that will only hurt her more than you already have today."

It seems Patrick is taking a moment to examine the metaphorical chess board. He must realize he only has one move left.

"As long as you know your place, we won't have a problem."

Even the old, shy Shelly never took a dressing down from anyone. This time is no different.

"My place is wherever she decides it to be. As long as you remember that, you might have a chance of keeping her. Maybe it will help your relationship to know that with one call, I will be there to sweep her off her feet if that's what she wants. Hell, I might be doing you a favor, forcing you to appreciate what you have. God knows you don't deserve her."

Patrick is quiet. I have a strong urge to peek at him to see if it's a moment of reflection or if his anger is building, but I don't want to get caught eavesdropping. When he does speak, his voice sounds quiet and resolved.

"I may have to accept you in her life as her friend, but I damn sure don't have to share our hotel room with you. Your time is up." I can't see him, but I imagine he's pointing toward the door.

Shelly bends down to kiss me on my head, and I hear Patrick growl. How these lunatics can honestly believe I'm still asleep through all this is beyond me.

"Bye, Dawson," Shelly whispers before his footsteps recede. The hotel room door opens and closes again, and Shelly is gone. There's another dip in the bed beside me, and I know it's Patrick as he leans down and presses the tip of his nose to mine.

"You heard all that, didn't you—you big faker."

I giggle, and it blows my cover. "Every word."

He grabs my body and pulls it closer to his, and I let out a happy sigh.

"I thought I lost you." His voice breaks with the emotion he's trying to hold back. "It scared the hell out of me, sweetheart. I am so sorry for not listening to you. Even if what happened was the worst thing that could have happened, I shouldn't have run off and left you behind. Please believe how sorry I am. I didn't know how to handle it. I told you from the start I wasn't good at this boyfriend thing, but I swear to God, I'm trying."

"I never want to go through that again. My heart broke today when you left, and I can't stand the thought of not being with you. Please don't ever walk away from me." I tell him earnestly.

He kisses me like a man who's searched the city for me all day. After our kiss, he brings his forehead down to rest against mine as he holds me close.

"I am yours, Dawson. One hundred percent yours. I had a lot of time to think while walking around the city today looking for you. My jealousy got the better of me. I realize that now, and that wasn't fair to you."

He hesitates before saying the rest of what he's thinking. "I also know that you went right from college to being married to the biggest jackass on Earth, and you went right from him to me."

I hold his face between my hands and look into his eyes. "I don't have any regrets, and I wouldn't change a thing. If I didn't go through all of what I went through, I might not have ended up with you."

Patrick looks tortured as he lets go and turns his head away from me. "I know you didn't get all the time you needed to be your own person outside of a relationship. If you need to work some things out of your system... If you need to have certain experiences with Levi Shelly..." He's struggling to finish his sentence, but I think I understand what he's offering.

"Patrick, are you trying to give me a hall pass?"

His eyes squint shut at the thought of it. "I'm trying to, but I don't know if I mean it. I don't want to share you, but more than that... I want to see you happy.

Damn it, baby, I'd do anything to make you happy. Even if... even if you wanted that experience with him. I'm not a big enough man to let you go completely, but maybe we could compromise."

My heart swells with love for this man. This is all I need, this strong alpha male being vulnerable in my arms. I'm the only one who gets this side of him, and I love it. That he has considered being okay with me having a night with Shelly blows my mind. He wants to put my happiness before his own, even though his attempt is somewhat misguided.

"You'd be alright if I had a night of wild sex with Shelly?"

He wraps me in his arms and holds me tightly to him, grunting at either the displeasure of the thought of me with another man or the pleasure of feeling my body closer to his.

"If it's what you need, I will do my best to understand. I will always respect you being your own person and making your own decisions, but make no mistake—I'm hoping like hell you turn down my offer."

He brings his mouth down to mine to give me a kiss hotter than a late afternoon New Orleans sidewalk. One of his hands roams down my thigh, and when it makes its way back up, it's under my dress. He plays with the string on the side of my swimsuit bottoms.

"You've worn this sexy-ass bikini all day?" His mouth leaves my lips and heads to my neck. He finds the sensitive spot right behind my ear and starts there as he kisses his way down.

"Yes, I've worn it all day," I say through his distractions. He pulls the string on the side and moves me to where he can do the same to the other side. In less than five seconds, he's got them off and is tossing them across the room.

"I underestimated how much I like your string bikini." With my bottoms gone, his head disappears under my dress. I grab the sheets with both my hands to help ground myself as his mouth finds its way between my legs.

He knows how good he is at this. He has a right to be as confident as he is. Within moments, I'm unabashedly writhing against him, and I don't care how desperate I seem as I get to the climax I'm chasing. I need him. I need this.

Today scared me, too. I let in the worry that he'd left me... No. I can't even think about my life without him. My grip on the sheets tightens as I try to hold myself together, knowing I'm about to come apart into a million tiny, happy pieces.

"I don't want Shelly—not like this. I only want you, and I want you to do this to me five times a day, every day. Can you agree to that?" I manage to say in between panting breaths.

I feel his laugh against the most inner part of me before he returns to his task. His hands slide up my stomach and under my bikini top. He can't get to the strings, so he pushes the cups above my breasts. His mouth works faster as his hands move in a massaging motion.

"I take your silence as assent!" I shout as I ride out one of the strongest orgasms I've ever had in my life.

By the time Patrick takes off his clothes and slides under the covers beside me, I'm practically purring. All my pent-up worries and frustrations are gone, and my body feels like melted butter.

I force energy back into my limbs to turn toward Patrick as I pull the sheet off his naked body. I take my time looking down the length of him before my eyes make it back to his.

I give him a saucy little smile. "Well, goodnight!" I kiss him on the shoulder and roll over to face the other side. I'm trying to hold back my laugh, but I can't hold in the giggles when he starts to tickle me.

"Goodnight? Really? How good a night is it?"

He keeps tickling me until I'm squirming to get away from him, and I'm laughing so hard tears are falling from my eyes. I swat playfully at his hands, but it's no use. With him behind me and my back to him, he's winning the tickle war. Finally, he stops and pulls me back into him.

"Every night I get to spend with you is a good night," he says as he kisses my temple. I turn and put my hand on his shoulder to push him back down onto the bed.

"You're in luck because tonight is about to go from good to great." I slide down his body to show him how glad I am to have him back.

9

The next morning, we wake up to a knock at the door, followed by an announcement that room service has arrived. I look over at Patrick, but he seems to have just woken up as well. I can't imagine he ordered us breakfast and went back to sleep.

"I'll tell them they've got the wrong room," Patrick says in a groggy voice as he stumbles his way to the door. He slips his jeans back on before he gets there to keep from giving the poor hotel worker an eye full of what I'm sure is his morning salute to the world.

"Sorry, buddy. Wrong room." Patrick is about to shut the door in his face when I hear the person on the other side.

"Is this Dawson Everly's room? Are you him?"

Patrick steps back where I can see him as he answers the person at the door. "No, I'm not 'him,' but don't worry. He's right here."

He twists his neck to look over at me. "I will never get used to you having a dude's name. We sound like a gay couple."

Patrick seems to realize what he's said and turns back to

the guy standing outside our door. Wanting to be sure this man doesn't think he's homophobic, he stumbles through an explanation. "Nothing wrong with that, of course. It's just, well, weird sometimes dating a woman with a masculine-sounding name. That's all."

They stare at each other for a moment, which only serves to ramp up the awkwardness.

I hear the guy outside break the silence by clearing his throat before saying, "I appreciate your open-minded views on sexuality, sir. If you don't mind, I have a delivery for Dawson Everly."

I cover my mouth with my hand to hold back my laugh.

Patrick looks back at me and points in the man's direction. "How did we get lucky enough to get the funny bellhop this early in the morning?"

I know he's trying to hide his embarrassment, but it has served a good enough purpose. Their banter has given me enough time to put on clothes and become somewhat decent. "Let the poor guy in. I'm sure he has other things he needs to get to today."

Patrick steps back, far enough for the young man to wheel in his cart. It's loaded down with two shelves of covered trays, and there is a rather large present wrapped in gold paper with a white and gold bow.

"Thank you," Patrick says as he tries to hand the guy a tip.

The man refuses it. "Sorry, sir. This has all been taken care of. Even the tip." He exits quietly, leaving Patrick, me, and all our questions alone in the room.

Patrick takes off the lids to find what seems like every kind of breakfast food imaginable hiding inside.

"Wonder who it's from?" I ask in a small voice, knowing there is zero chance it's from anybody else but Shelly.

Pour Boy

Patrick looks at me with a cocked eyebrow. "We both know who it's from and if it didn't smell so damn good, I'd hate him for it."

I hand him one of the plates and start selecting some of the goodies for myself. "At least he sent enough for both of us."

Despite his surly attitude, Patrick's face brightens when he notices the carafe of coffee, and we manage to eat our breakfast in companionable silence.

I half expected him to toss the whole thing out the window—cart and all—when we realized what it was and who it came from. I'm impressed he's controlling himself, even though he glances back at the offending cart every minute or two. If he is mentally trying to calculate how much force he needs or the swing radius he'd have to use to launch it through the double-paned glass like a rocket ship, at least he's not verbalizing it.

Patrick looks back at the cart again, and I put my fork down on my plate with a loud clang.

"Something I can get for you?"

Yes, I know this must be hard for him, but it was nice of Shelly to do this. And Patrick isn't the only one who can be grumpy in the morning.

"He got you a present. There's a gift on the bottom of the cart. That is, I'm assuming it's for you and not me. I didn't see a tag."

"And it was very nice of him. So is this breakfast we're still trying to enjoy." I pick up my fork in a not-so-subtle hint for him to put his jealous monster back in its cage and enjoy the damn food.

His eyes wander back to the present again before picking up his fork. He doesn't resume eating. Instead, he stares down at his plate for a while before saying, "If there is a miniature picnic basket in there, I'm going to lose my shit."

I bark out a laugh. I can't help it. That was what Mack had given me after I told him in no uncertain terms that I wanted a divorce.

"I'm sure there's no dime store token of undying love in that gift box. Shelly is not my ex-husband. I mean, we've got to assume with his money, it's probably way better than a miniature picnic basket."

I needle him on purpose just because it's fun. Patrick lets out a loud, disgruntled harumph.

"Besides, the box is much too big to only have a little old, crappy knickknack in it."

Okay, that didn't help. He stares at me to let me know he doesn't appreciate my speculations.

I can tell we will not be able to move forward until I open the gift. The problem is that it could very well be a token of Shelly's undying love for me. This makes me hesitant to rip that puppy open in front of Patrick, but it's not like I'm left with another option. Sooner or later, I'm going to have to bite the bullet. I might as well get it over with now.

"Here goes nothing." I stand up and walk across the room to get the present. I try to open it with my back to him, but Patrick figures out what I'm doing and comes to stand beside me.

I pull the ribbon, take off the paper, and open the large box to find several smaller presents wrapped inside.

Patrick sighs into my ear when he sees it. "Oh, goodie. There's more."

I take a thin present off the top and open it, noticing several pieces of paper inside. The first one is a save-the-date card for Shelly's next book launch party, several months away. It has the date, location, and a note to let the reader know to expect a formal invitation in the future. Patrick reads it over my shoulder.

"Huh. No wonder he had the pull to get this hotel room put in his name and out of mine. He's having his book launch party here."

Should I tell him Shelly changed all his original plans for his book launch just so I could grab my purse? It may make him feel worse about yesterday, so I decide against it. Underneath the invitation is a voucher for a two-week stay at the French Royal Inn along with the invoice from our current stay, both paid in full.

"This guy has got a lot of nerve already, and we haven't even opened the rest of these things yet. Who the hell does he think he is? He thinks I can't pay for my damn hotel room? Motherfuc—"

"Stop it." I give him some serious side-eye. "It's thoughtful, and I'm sure now that he has the ability to do things like this, it makes him very happy."

"Uh-huh."

I reach in and open the next box. Inside is a leatherbound notebook. Embossed on the front cover is a waxing crescent moon with wings sprouting up from each side. The wings are made of ivy.

"This is beautiful." I run a reverent hand over the cover.

Patrick's voice is incredulous. "Isn't that the same damn tattoo the man has below his navel? The one you looked like you were trying to lick?"

He's trying not to be, but I can tell he's angry. Patrick starts to find a shirt and shoes to put on so he can go do God knows what, but I grab his arm and bring my big, hulking man back to where we were standing.

"I wasn't trying to lick anything. Look, it's a long story

and not as illicit as what you're thinking right now. So, I'll ask you again. Do you trust me?"

Patrick puffs out a hard breath and looks up at the ceiling.

"I can trust you and still kill him, right?"

I can tell he's mad as hell but trying to hold it together.

"No, you can't." I pick up the second to last gift. Inside the box is a large manila envelope, and I open it to find a stack of typed sheets of paper. When my eyes recognize what I'm holding, I gasp.

It's my story.

The thick stack of papers trembles in my hand, and I walk backward to the bed until I can sit down. "I can't believe he still has this!"

"Has what?" Patrick asks in desperation to understand anything that is going on at the moment.

A Post-it note in Shelly's handwriting is stuck to the front page. All these years later, I can still recognize it on sight, and even that makes me emotional.

The note says, "I made you a copy. I'm not ready to let go of the original."

Tears slide down my face as I read his note and the first few lines of a story I'd written so long ago. The fact that this meant so much to him, that something I wrote inspired all his success, is both awe-inspiring and humbling. As I read through a few paragraphs, I realize I do miss this part of myself more than I ever thought I would. I try to wipe away my tears without letting the moisture hit the paper.

"Are you going to tell me what is happening?" Patrick asks in a softer voice. Crying Dawson scares him, but he's concerned about me and more than curious as to what everything means.

I know I need to tell him about all this, but not until the end, not until I've opened all the gifts. I want to see what else is in store before I let him in on this part of me.

Even though he isn't here—right now I'm sharing this moment with Shelly.

"One more to go," I tell Patrick instead of answering him. He seems to give up because he walks back to his chair at our breakfast table and sits down.

I reach inside and grab the last present. It takes up the entire bottom part of the box it came in, and I have a sneaking suspicion as to what it is before I unwrap it.

I'm right.

Patrick stands up to see what I have in my hands. His eyes narrow before he closes them again and takes a deep breath. "Dawson, why did he buy you a laptop? You know what? Say it to me. Say, 'Patrick, this old friend of mine is not trying to get in my pants by buying me an expensive-looking laptop.'"

I can't say that because I don't think it's true. Shelly outright confessed his feelings for me, so I know he wants to be with me—although I don't think that was his main goal in giving me this laptop. I believe he simply wants me to write again.

There's a larger note on top than the last gift had, and I tune out Patrick long enough to read it.

My Dearest Dawson,

I know you already have a computer, and though I don't know what kind you have, I can promise you this one is better. Every serious writer needs a trusty steed on which to charge into battle. Tell Patrick to calm down. I'm not trying to buy your affection. All of this is a mere deposit toward paying you back for everything you've done for me. When I was homeless, you gave me shelter. When I was hungry, you fed me (ramen noodles), and when my soul needed to be heard, you listened with yours. I can never repay you for all you've given me. Though I cannot hold your heart, I still have you as my friend and my muse. May your fingers be reckless as they fly across this keyboard to construct and create your own universes, and I hope you do so in the secure knowledge that I believe in you with everything I am."

Love,
Levi Shelly

"Damn," I say in a whisper.

"That's it!" Patrick shouts as he shoves the last shoe on his foot. I step into his path and put my hand on his heaving chest.

"What are you doing?"

He tries to move around me, but I won't let him.

"What am I doing? I'm headed to rip that motherfucker's head off!"

I can almost see the steam rolling out of his ears. "I've already told Shelly he doesn't have a chance with me. You don't need to go over there."

"He didn't listen to you, so I'm going to say it louder." He tries to get by me, but I keep blocking his path.

"Stop being a caveman! Do you remember yesterday when you didn't allow me to explain? How did that work out for you?"

He stops trying to get by me. After a moment of thought, he moves to the side and placatingly holds an out arm, inviting me to sit back down at our breakfast table. "By all means, please explain like I've asked you to do all morning. Take your time. The room's paid for." He walks over to his chair and sits down.

"You can start by looking at this." I plop my thick stack of pages in his hands.

"Pure Midnight." He reads the title aloud and then scans the first page to himself. His eyes roll in his head before they make their way to me.

"If you tell me this asshat wrote you a froo-froo novel to woo you away from me, you won't be able to stop me from walking out that door. I'm trying not to let him get to me, but this is too much. I told you if you want him, I won't stand in your way, but please don't make me sit by and do nothing while he comes after you with everything he's got. That's not who I am, sweetheart."

"I wrote that novel."

His eyes bulge out of his head for a moment before they return to the pages in his hands.

He tries to backpedal. "I didn't mean froo-froo, I meant... amazing. I'm sure this is an amazing novel. Um, when did you write a novel? And why don't I know this about you?"

I smile at him. "Because I'm an enigma—full of secrets and wrapped in mystery, Mr. Butler. You don't know everything about me."

"I know you're sexy enough to have any man you want, and even though I understand Shelly wanting to shoot his shot, this needs to stop."

I crawl onto his lap, straddling him. I hold his head in my hands so he will look at me.

"I won't apologize for Shelly being my friend. He's helped me find a piece of myself I had lost, and I'm grateful. That being said, you are the man I choose. You are who I want to be with, to wake up to every morning—my grumpy, curmudgeonly, jealous monster of a man."

He sets my novel down and tickles my ribs as I say the last part, and I wiggle around laughing. He's laughing, too, because he knows both parts are true. He is the man I choose, and he can be a grumpy curmudgeon, who I still want to be with every day of my life.

"I love you, Dawson," he says as he holds me tighter. My eyebrows shoot up in surprise. He's not drunk like he was the other night. He's stone-cold sober and holding me like he will never let me go. I'm about to say it back like I've wanted to do for so long, but I have a better idea.

"Get in line."

It takes him a second to catch what I mean. When he does, his eyes widen, and his mouth falls open in surprise. "Oh, no, you didn't!" He laughs at my joke and tickles me harder. I'm glad he can have a sense of humor about everything, and I hope it means we're over this particular hump.

"Sorry, babe. I couldn't resist."

He stops his tickle assault, and I reach up to wipe my eyes from laughing so hard. Once I've calmed down, I look at this man who means everything to me.

"Patrick, I love you, too. You know I do." I lean in and give him a soft kiss. "You're mine, I'm yours, and I wouldn't have it any other way."

"What's that?" I ask as Patrick returns to the room carrying two plastic bags on his arm. They look full, but I can't tell what's in them.

"You'll see. I have my secrets, too, Dr. Everly. He gives me a quick kiss before putting the last few items he had left to pack in his suitcase and zipping it up.

We spent our last few days in New Orleans touring the city together. At night, we curled up in bed, and I read Patrick a few chapters from my book. We're breathing new life into the part of me I thought would never see the light of day again, and I'm eager to share this piece of myself with him.

Our trip may have started off rocky, but it ended up being magical. I'm sad it's coming to an end because I have loved being in New Orleans with my man.

As I roll my suitcases to the door, I think about what an amazing adventure this was. It was our first vacation together as a couple, and it's one for the history books. My friends back home won't believe me when I tell them what happened, so I might keep some of it to myself. It might be best if a certain portion stays between Patrick and me... and maybe a smaller fraction between Shelly and me. There were good and bad parts, but overall, I'm glad to have made these memories.

Except for my phone call to Shelly to thank him for my gifts, I haven't heard from him. I think about calling him several times throughout the rest of the week while we're still in the city, but instead, I choose to put him out of my mind and enjoy my vacation with the man I love.

When I get back to Starkford, I'll reach out to Shelly again and start rebuilding our friendship to what it should be because I meant what I said. I don't want to lose him from my life again. He'll eventually understand I'm not giving up Patrick for him or anybody else. Then maybe I can have it all... the man I love and my old best friend.

"Ready?" Patrick asks me as we start our convoy of suitcases toward the front of the hotel.

"As I'll ever be."

Patrick has already called for our car to be brought around, so it's parked and waiting when we walk out the front door. I start to head to the passenger's seat, but he stops me.

"Where are you going?"

I point to the seat I was about to occupy. A fleeting thought runs through my brain of how he might still be mad and expect me to find my own way home, but that's a stupid, invasive thought born out of fear, paranoia, and having been married to the wrong man for years. I know Patrick, and he would never do that to me. This man loves me. He told me so himself.

"I think you'll be needing these." He drops the keys into my hands and leads me to the driver's side door.

"What? You mean you're going to let me drive your precious Beverly?"

He laughs at my melodramatic question. "You can call her Bev. We had a talk, and she likes you enough to let you in her driver's seat for a little while. Also, I got you this."

He hands me the two plastic bags, filled to the brim with what looks like every item from the hotel vending machine, along with a few sodas. I look up at him, confused.

"Are you trying to cut down on my driving time by forcing me into a diabetic coma?"

"No, I gave you a hard time about eating and drinking in my vehicle on our way down here, and I want to show you I can do better. I also want to show you I'm not the only extravagant man in your life." He's poking fun at Shelly's presents to me, and I don't mind one bit.

"That's my big spender," I joke as I set the bags on the seat and pull him in for a long kiss.

Pour Boy

The valets and a few passersby whistle catcalls at us, and I hear one person yell out, "Get a room!"

Patrick breaks the kiss long enough to yell back, "Already had one. We just checked out!" before coming right back in to finish our scorching hot kiss on the scorching hot sidewalk in the scorching hot city of New Orleans.

10

Patrick and I are in his car and heading to his father's house for Wednesday Card Night when my phone vibrates with an incoming call.

I read the screen before I answer. "Hey, Shelly. How's it going?"

I haven't heard from him in the month or so since we've been back from New Orleans, so I sent him a text yesterday. When he didn't respond, I was sure I'd never hear from him again.

Patrick rolls his eyes. "Please tell Shelly that the man you love, who is sitting right here beside you, says hello."

I laugh as he playfully squeezes my leg. "Patrick says hello."

"Oh, I heard him. Is he behaving? Treating you right? Do you need to put me on speakerphone?"

These men are going to be the death of me. "Everything is perfect. Did you see my text yesterday?"

Patrick shoots me a sideways look. I hope he doesn't think I'm going to tell him every time I text my friend because there is no way that's happening.

"I did see it, but I don't think I understand it. I want to apologize for not contacting you sooner. Honestly, I felt bad for how strongly I came on to you when you were down here, so I was planning to give you some space before reaching back out. However, your text has me very intrigued. Explain more, please."

I'm glad to hear he's curious about my master plan. This is the reaction I was hoping to get from him.

"Certainly. A friend of mine came up with a great idea we think would be perfect for you. I don't know if you've ever been to Starkford, but I live in the cutest little college town."

"I haven't, but go on."

"There's an old, rundown opera house here that could be made into a fabulous events venue with a little renovation... and it wouldn't be a bad tax write-off, either."

"Theater, huh? Besides books, our company has branched off into movies, television, and music, but we've not gotten into theater yet."

I don't need to get excited because that was a long way from a yes, but I like that "yet" he added to the end of his sentence.

"Do you think Shelly Brothers, Inc. would be interested? It could be a non-profit organization in partnership with Bellhurst College, where I work."

Patrick pretends to bang his head on the steering wheel, and I laugh at him. If he had known how close Shelly and I used to be, he would know there was little-to-no likelihood of this man not being in my life, as a friend, from here on out.

I google the theater and shoot Shelly some images. Even though it needs a lot of love, it's still a beauty.

"I've gotten to where I am today because I'm not quick to

say no. Oh, I just got the pictures. This might not be a terrible idea. We could even debut some of our movies there, and with my brother Liam's music connections, we could keep the place packed year-round. Hmm."

"So, is that a yes?"

He laughs at my eagerness. I have driven by this gorgeous old place countless times since I moved here and would love to see it brought back to life. Truth be told, I would have never thought of Shelly investing in it had it not been for Nate, one of the bartenders at Study.

Nate has just graduated with his bachelor's degree in business and is having a hard time finding a job that pays enough. If he got in on a new business from the ground up, he could get his salary where it needs to be faster. Plus, he minored in theater, so it's perfect. I'll have to tell Shelly about Nate later. I don't want Patrick turning against one of his best bartenders on my account.

"Let me talk to my family, run some numbers, and I'll let you know." He pauses for a moment before adding, "But if we do go forward with it, I already have the perfect name picked out."

"Oh, yeah, what's that?"

"The Everly."

Shit. Patrick's going to love that. Shelly doesn't wait for my response. "Did you get the official invitation to my book launch?"

What? I haven't seen an invitation to anything from him. "No, somehow I must have missed that piece of mail." I turn my head slowly to look toward Patrick. He shrugs his shoulders, but his smile lets me know there's a reason I didn't receive it. And that reason is currently driving me to his dad's house.

Shelly must have known from my tone that Patrick had

something to do with the missing invitation. "No worries, from now on, I'll send everything to your office. I do hope you can come, and you can even bring that Neanderthal with you. I bet he's fun to hang out with when he's not trying to murder me."

"He is a good time." I reach over and pinch Patrick's cheek.

He strains his neck to get out of my reach. "Woman, I'm driving here. Safety first."

"I have a room booked under your name in case you can make it."

"You don't have to—" I start to say, but he cuts me off.

"Are you writing?"

"Is this going to be a question you ask every single time we talk to each other from now until we die?"

"Yes."

I sigh into the phone. "Fine. I'm flirting with it. I wouldn't call what I'm doing right now 'writing,' but it's definitely foreplay."

Patrick raises one eyebrow and slowly turns his head to look at me. Having heard only one side of the conversation, I can see where he's confused.

"Dude, eyes on the road. Safety first!"

He mutters something unintelligible but focuses back on the road instead of me.

"So, tell me, are you doing something that scares you? How are you putting yourself out there?" If Shelly is going to ask me the writing question until the end of time, I need one to ask him in return.

"Actually, I am. You're talking to the new adjunct professor at Belle Rive University."

"You're going to be teaching?"

"If Matthew McConaughey can do it, so can I. I start this

fall with just one class. See, Dawson—you're still my inspiration."

"That's awesome! You're going to be the best professor they've ever had."

Patrick turns into his dad's driveway, and I know it's time I end this conversation. "Shel, can I call you tomorrow? I've got to run."

"You can call me anytime, and I mean that. I miss you, my friend."

"I miss you, too. I'll talk to you tomorrow."

I hang up, but neither of us makes a move to get out of the car. I'm too chicken to turn and look at Patrick's face.

"Are you okay?"

Through my peripheral vision, I can see his hands are still clutching the steering wheel.

"I'm jealous."

I feel like a broken record, but I tell him again. "Shelly and I are just friends. That's all."

"I know that. In my brain, I know that. The problem is that this caveman who lives inside me doesn't know that."

"So... Can we maybe tell him, too?"

Patrick turns to face me. "There's only one language he understands."

He pulls me to him and slants his mouth over mine. I open for him, and his kiss is raw with passion and need. He grabs me under my arms and hauls me across the center console until he sits me in his lap, straddling him. The space is tight and awkward, but with his hands on my body, I don't care that we're dry-humping like teenagers in his dad's driveway. I want him.

He makes a low moaning sound as I grind down on him. I can feel his hardness against my center, and it makes me want to do crazy, reckless things.

"I love you, Dawson Everly. I love you with everything inside of me." He pulls my hips down, making me rub harder against him, and we both groan at the sensation it gives us.

"I love you too, Patrick. I always have, and I always will." I mean that, and I hope he knows it.

I'd be lying if I said I never thought about what it would be like to take Shelly up on his offer to be with him or even Patrick's offer for me to have him for a night. It's a fun daydream, but that's all it is. I have no interest in blowing up what is real and wonderful for a work of fiction.

Had I still been with Mack, I would be packing my bags and moving to New Orleans because I would have nothing to lose. With Patrick, I would lose everything. I would lose my whole heart because it belongs to him. This man—who said he didn't know how to love—loves me harder and better than anyone ever has. I'll take the jealous caveman because it means I also get the passionate, untamed lover in my bed. With Patrick, there's not one without the other, but if I'm honest, I love his jealous caveman side just as much as the rest of him.

He fists his hand in the back of my hair and pulls me to him for a kiss I feel down to my toes. I'm about to tell him to drive us back home when we jump apart at a knock on his window.

"Children, let's stop trying to eat each other's faces off and come inside."

I put my hand on my heart to stop it from racing as I realize it's his dad who has scared the living shit out of us.

My head drops into my hands, and it muffles my voice. "Hi, Henry."

I'm mortified Patrick's dad caught us simulating sex in

his front yard. We've steamed up the windows, but I'm sure he has a pretty good idea what's going on.

"Hello, Dawson, dear. Do you need help climbing off my son?" He is getting such a kick out of finding us like this, but I think I may die of embarrassment.

Patrick hits the button to let the window down, and I put my face in the nook where his shoulder meets his neck in a feeble and pointless attempt to hide.

"Father, why don't you give us a minute? We'll be right behind you," he says slowly, almost in a threatening way to let his dad know he's not playing right now.

"Oh, take your time. I'm just messing with you two. Besides, I'd love to have more grandbabies, so keep up the good work."

I look up in time to see Henry giving us a thumbs-up as he takes off back toward the house.

Patrick slams his head back onto his headrest and closes his eyes in frustration as he hits the button for the window to roll back up. "Sorry about his baby comment. He doesn't know the struggles you've had in the past."

When Mack and I were trying to get pregnant, he made me feel like something was wrong with me for not being able to conceive. Honestly, the whole marriage was traumatizing, but that part stung worse than the rest of it.

"Do you want to have children?" I'm hesitant to ask, knowing if the answer is yes, I might not be able to give them to him. If that's the case, could I let him go? Could I follow his example and offer to put his happiness before my own? I don't know if I could.

"Sweetheart, I would love for you to have my child—my children. I never thought I'd want them, but that life with you sounds perfect."

I look down. He puts his hand under my chin and raises

my head, so I'll look at him again. "But if there are issues where we aren't able to do that, and you decide you want children, we'll find a way. I don't want you worrying for a second about this. As long as I'm with you, I'm happy. You are enough for me. Everything else is a bonus."

He reaches into the console to grab one of his neatly stacked napkins so I can wipe under my eyes. He couldn't have known how worried about this I've been since we've been together, but he did. He did know and is saying all the right things. Better than that, I believe he means them.

Patrick opens the car door, and I inelegantly climb off him and out of the car. Maybe I could have used Henry's help after all. He gets out after I do, and I'm making my way to his dad's front door when Patrick gets my attention.

"Sweetheart, I think you dropped something."

I pat the pockets of my jeans. I have my phone, and I don't recall bringing anything else with me.

"No, I didn't."

He holds out his hand, insistent I take whatever it is he picked up.

"Fine." I open my hand, and he drops something into it. When I look at it, I see it's a key.

"No, that's not mine. I didn't bring any keys, especially a loose one. When we get inside, we can ask Henry and Jameson if they're missing one."

He grabs my hand as I start to turn, keeping me with him. "No, I'm pretty sure it's yours."

"Why are you being weird?"

"I'm not being weird." He pulls out his keys and finds the one on the ring he's looking for. He takes the one I'm holding out of my hand and puts them together. "See? I have my house key. This one must be yours."

I step closer to examine the keys. I take them from his

hands and turn them at different angles, inspecting them. "They're identical."

"Exactly. I have my house key, so this one... must be yours."

"Patrick, what do you—"

I stop when he gets down on one knee in front of me.

"Dawson, I want more than anything for us to be together for the rest of our lives. I know you just got out of a horrible marriage, and I know you need time to recover from that. I also know what we have between us has been a whirlwind, but it's the best thing that has ever happened to me. You need to know I will marry you tomorrow if that's what you want. I'm all in, but at the same time, I don't want to rush you."

"Oh, Patrick—"

He raises his hand and smiles at me. "Hang on, sweetheart. I've practiced this in the mirror and want to be sure I say everything right."

I laugh at that. "Please, continue."

"I needed to find a way to let you know how much I love you and want to be with you without scaring the daylights out of you and having you running for the hills. That's why I waited so long to tell you how I feel about you, but you need to know I have felt it every moment since we met.

One day soon, a ring will be in my hand when I'm down on one knee. Today, it's a key. This gives you all the control. You can use it as much or as little as you'd like. I'm hoping for "much," and if that's your choice, I can have you moved out of the cottage and into my house by tomorrow afternoon. However, if you choose "little," I'm okay with that, too. You've got my heart along with that key, and I'll never ask for either of them back."

I drop down to my knees and throw my arms around

him. I'm crying and laughing, filled with so much happiness I think I might burst. "Much! I choose much."

"Really?" His face is beaming. "You're going to move in with me?"

"I am."

He grabs me and pulls me closer, bringing his head down to give me a searing kiss that hints at what he wants us to be doing when we get back... to our home.

"We may never leave the house again."

I raise an eyebrow at him. "You say that like it's a bad thing."

He stands up before reaching down to pull me to my feet and starts brushing the dirt off our jeans. Looking toward the house, I see Henry and Jameson peeking through the window. Their heads quickly disappear when they see I've caught them spying on us.

I realize what they must have seen if they've been watching us for a while out their window. "Patrick, your family thinks we just got engaged."

He laughs deeply at that, and it's a nice sound. We're both laughing more these days than we did before we found each other, but Patrick was right. For me, it's too soon to get married. I'm not even sure I believe in it anymore. My commitment to this man is real, and that's all that matters.

"We should tell them that's not what just happened."

Patrick leans over and kisses me on the forehead before we reach the front porch. "Nah, I love keeping secrets from them. It's one of my favorite things to do. Did I ever tell you about buying Study?"

I shake my head at him as he knocks on the front door.

"I'll tell you later. All you need to know now is to win the game, they have to admit they were spying. Other than that, there are no rules."

"Do they know we're playing a game?"

"Oh, yeah. They know. We're always playing a game. Dawson, welcome to the Butler family."

Henry opens the door with a wide grin on his face, and I walk inside to spend the evening with the man I love and his crazy, wonderfully dysfunctional family. I grab Patrick's hand as we walk through the house to the kitchen. It's no fancy party in a New Orleans mansion, but I wouldn't have it any other way. To me, it's perfect.

Jameson is shuffling the cards at the kitchen table. He gives me a big smile when he sees us walk in, but he doesn't say anything about what he saw. Instead, he looks over at Patrick. "It's your turn to be in charge of the music."

He points his chin to the counter where Henry's small stereo sits with an auxiliary cord hanging out.

Patrick wraps his arms around me from behind and brings his head around to give me a sweet kiss on the cheek. "Oh, perfect! I know just what to play since Dawson has a new favorite band."

"I do?" I move my head to where I can see his face, and he looks so pleased with himself.

"Yep. All she wants to hear these days is the Foggy Holler Mountain Cats."

NOTE FROM THE AUTHOR

Were you sad Dawson didn't end up with Levi Shelly? I get it. A little part of me was, too.

Though I knew Patrick was Dawson's soul mate, it was impossible not to fall in love with Shelly and root for him to win the girl of his dreams—even when I knew her heart would forevermore belong to Mr. Patrick Butler.

But guess what... Okay, stop guessing. I'll tell you.

I'm writing Levi's book next. Maybe my Gatsby will be able to find the love he's wanted all these years, or maybe his crazy brothers will drive him certifiably insane. Who knows? (I do, but I'm not telling—yet).

Stay tuned!

ALSO BY P.J. DEVERE

Pour Choices

Pour House

Pour Attitude

Pour Baby

ABOUT THE AUTHOR

P.J. DeVere writes contemporary romance filled with spice and sass. As a life-long lover of books, she finds it hard to tear herself away from a steamy romance novel.

She is a wonderful wife, a terrible housekeeper, and a devoted mother. Her sons are all grown with lives of their own, and she is making use of this newfound time and freedom to get to know the imaginary friends in her head.

P.J. has had multiple careers in her life, but writing is by far her favorite. Before earning her law degree from Ole Miss and becoming an attorney, she was a fifth-grade teacher. Besides her law degree, she has a bachelor's degree in elementary education and a master's degree in curriculum and instruction.

Her decade in college notwithstanding, P.J. will vehemently argue to anyone that writing her 'dirty books' has been and continues to be the most efficient and productive use of her time and talent.

Learn more about her books at: www.pjdevere.com

- facebook.com/P.J.DeVere.author
- instagram.com/p.j.devere
- tiktok.com/@pjdevere
- amazon.com/author/pjdevere
- bookbub.com/authors/p-j-devere

Made in the USA
Monee, IL
08 May 2025

17116032R00069